316: A Story of 1920s M
John Brock

Copyright 2018 by John Brock

All rights reserved, including the right to reproduce this book, or portions thereof, in any format whatsoever.

The characters and events in this book are fictitious or are used fictitiously. Any similarities to real persons, living or dead, are purely coincidental and not intended by the author.

To Ruth, my wife, and Anna, my mother, the two most wonderful women in the world

Acknowledgements

EVERYTHING I HAVE READ about acknowledgements is to keep them short. So here goes.

I could not have done this without my three editors, Valerie Borders, Jen Gabel, and Steve Medlin. Valerie, thank you for affirming that the story worked. Jen, thank you for reminding me to make the reader feel like they are there. Steve, thank you for showing me that the characters needed a bit more depth. So to my editors, I couldn't have done it without you.

To my wife Ruth, thank you for letting me drag you to a U2 concert in Miami, which allowed me to experience the city that inspired this work. I know you thought I would never finish it, but here it is!

To my friends and students, your excitement that I was writing a book helped me get to this point. Thank you for that encouragement.

Well, I know I left many out who were so helpful and encouraging, but brevity is often what I do. So all I can say is thank you! You know who you are.

Prologue
The Terms

THE WHIRRING MOTOR of the ceiling fan hummed into the open space as silence reigned at the circular table. Seated in wooden Shaker chairs across from each other, the husband and wife each sipped from their drink, Coca-Cola for the husband, tea for the wife. While he looked down at his drink, she stared toward him appraisingly, hoping to see some type of remorse. An oppressive silence hung over the room as neither was ready for the conversation ahead.

Finally, the husband spoke up, "How was the trip to Knoxville?"

"How do you think the trip to Knoxville was?" The wife said spitefully.

"I'm glad you decided to come back home."

"I still haven't decided if I'm staying."

"Oh."

The husband grabbed the wet Coca-Cola bottle from the table, wishing he had some whiskey to put into it, but knowing that he had to stay sober tonight. The wife looked up at him and shook her head angrily.

"I was away a month and all you want to ask about is how my trip to Knoxville was?"

The husband looked remorseful as he kept his eyes looking at the table instead of up at his wife.

She continued, "Before this year, if someone had asked me to describe my husband in one word, I would have said 'Loyal.' Now that's nothing but a joke to me."

"How many times do I have to say I made a terrible decision that I sincerely regret and I'm sorry?" the husband said distraught.

"One more time won't hurt," she quipped.

"I'm sorry," he said, looking up into her eyes and imploring her to understand his remorse.

Silence once again enveloped the room as each contemplated their next move as if they were two boxers circling the ring. The wife got up to refresh her tea, while the husband slowly nursed his cola. He pulled out his pipe and packed the tobacco in before lighting it. He drug the smoke into his mouth as she sat back down and asked, "If I am going to stay, this is going to be the last conversation we have about this."

"Fine with me," he responded hopefully.

She looked at him sternly, "Not so fast because I have several terms which you must agree to or I will pack up and the kids and I will move to Knoxville."

He looked at her for a moment before taking another taste from the pipe. "I'm willing to do whatever you wish."

"Well, I wish you would have been faithful, but I guess I don't get that wish."

The husband blushed red, but knew he deserved it. "What are your terms?"

She looked at him and put her elbows onto the table, leaning in. "First, I want to ask a few questions, and you will be completely honest with me. If I think you are lying, I'm done."

"Understood."

"Do you love her?"

Swallowing the lump that had formed in his throat, "Yes."

"More than me?"

"Different than you," he sighs as he looks down, admitting more than he wanted to.

"Bastard," She muttered.

She looked warily at him but continued.

"Have you heard from her since you returned?"

"No, nor have I tried to contact her."

She rocks in her chair before asking, "Do you want to see her again?"

He rubbed his hands across his face towards his ears before responding, "Honestly I don't know what I feel about that."

"Thank you for being honest."

He nodded, but said nothing before having another puff from the pipe.

"My next term is this: You cannot try to contact her in any way, shape or form ever again."

"Agreed," he said readily.

She took a sip of her tea before going into the next term.

"Third, I want us to stay in Charlottesville, so there will be no searching for other jobs. You are going to have to accept that you will spend the rest of your career here. When you are ready to retire, we can perhaps discuss moving then."

He nodded as he took a sip of Coca-Cola. She got up from the table and went into the kitchen and over to the icebox, grabbing another cola for him. She also stopped by the counter, and after popping the top off of the bottle, she picked up a piece of paper.

Walking back into the dining room, she silently handed the cola to him before sitting back into her chair.

Looking at the paper, she said, "Fourth, you will no longer submit papers or go to conventions. You have established yourself here and no longer need to be a part of the national community. Furthermore, as I need time to trust you again, I am not letting you out of my grasp again."

Sitting up straighter and looking her in the eye, he responded, "Wait a minute. I am more than willing to accept that I will be the professor of Southern History at University of Virginia for the next 30 years, but I have to be able to publish. I have to be able to go speak at conventions. I'm good at it! This is what fulfills me."

The wife thought to herself, *Well you should have thought about that before you decided to fulfill something else!* but instead said, "Fifth, I don't want anyone else to ever know what happened. I want everything about the trip erased. I will burn the letters you sent me. I want you to burn the program. Anything involved with the trip has to be thrown out. We will try to move forward the best we can, but in order to do that, we need to erase this from our history."

"I will never speak of it again. It'll be like it never happened."

The fan whirred as the wife leaned back in her chair and looked at the blades turning.

"Well, what's your answer? Do you accept my terms or not?" She asked, never looking away from the fan.

"Of course, I'd do anything to make this right," he said leaning forward and touched her arm lightly. She stiffened at his touch but looked softly into his eyes. He gave her a tentative smile.

Both fell silent as he looked out of the window toward the lamp-lit street where a 1925 Model T charged into the night.

Part I
Saturday, January 5, 1924

Chapter 1
The Train

AS THE TRAIN GROUND to a halt in the Union Terminal in Jacksonville, Dr. James Pashen took out a pinch of tobacco and packed his pipe tightly. He lit the pipe with a match and began to taste the smoke while casually glancing at the menu in the dining car, trying to figure out what he wanted for breakfast.

Normally an early riser, he had awakened with the sun somewhere between Savannah and Jacksonville, hungry for bacon and eggs from Maude's kitchen. He realized Maude's cooking was one of the many comforts from home he would do without for the next week. James examined the menu more closely, when a bald waiter in a bowtie interrupted his thoughts and asked him what he would like to drink.

"Milk, please," James responded as he tried to decide on the rest of his breakfast. James knew the milk would be fresh since the train just stopped and would be in Jacksonville for another 30 minutes. James finally decided he would have some fried eggs with muffins, then grabbed a newspaper that had just been brought on board.

James smiled when he noticed the date on the newspaper was today. Taking off his glasses, he tuned out the rest of the dining car while he began to read about President Coolidge's latest actions. However, this isolated peace was short-lived.

"James, my good man!" Erupted from the mouth of a white-haired man with bushy eyebrows. "I was hoping to see you here!"

"You know only the birth of a child would keep me from the conference, Walter," James responded without looking up from his newspaper.

Walter Shafer, a long-time colleague and friend who was now a professor at Harvard, took the empty seat at the table without an invitation and began trying to distract James from his newspaper. "So are we going to have a fun week in Miami?" Walter asked him.

"Maybe after I get done giving my speech on Monday. I'm presenting for the first time," James responded, still reading the newspaper.

"Well? What is it about?" Walter prodded, having not exchanged letters since the summer.

A bit frustrated at being interrupted, James hid it well as he began to expound on the importance of yeoman farmers in the antebellum South.

After a few minutes of James's explanation, Walter asked, "So when on Monday is the speech?"

"11:00," James responded.

"The right before lunch keynote?" Walter exclaimed, raising his bushy eyebrows, impressed that his former colleague was giving a keynote speech.

James sheepishly declared, "Yes."

"That's copacetic!" Walter answered. "I'd be proud of you if I wasn't so jealous!"

James just shrugged, trying not to feel the nervousness that was overwhelming him.

Walter continued, "So this speech will open a lot of new doors for you. Am I finally going to be able to convince you to come to an Ivy League school and be nearby?"

"I don't know. It certainly is a huge opportunity to have my work respected in the academic community, but Maude is happy in Charlottesville. We will just have to see."

"Speaking of Maude, how is the family?"

"She's good. They're good," James said automatically. "They will be spending the week with her parents in Tennessee while I am enjoying the sunny Florida weather."

"Sounds like she got the short end of the stick, traveling to Knoxville while you get to bask in the beaches of Miami."

"It will be rather cold, but she loves Knoxville and hasn't seen her parents in months. Her dad is actually about to retire as chair from the department there," James said.

"Any chance you might replace him?" Walter asked.

"I doubt it," James responded without any real feeling.

Walter looked at him appraisingly as James went back to his newspaper. Walter decided to let the conversation go and began to scan the room looking either for people he knew or women he could feed a line to.

After a few minutes of companionable silence, the waiter arrived to take the men's orders. James began to order when a friend of Walter's walked over to the table. James stood while Walter made the introductions.

"Hugh!" Walter smiled brightly. "This is James Pashen, professor of southern history at the University of Virginia. James, Hugh Campbell, professor of religious history at Princeton." As the men shook hands, James noticed Campbell's smile was more like a smirk, but he quickly realized his smile was genuine.

"So Dr. Campbell," James asked as they all sat down, "if you are at Princeton and you're last name is Campbell, does that make you Presbyterian?"

"Why yes it does, Dr. Pashen."

James, perking up as he always did when he realized someone was Presbyterian, began to ask Hugh about Princeton and his work on George Whitfield. Walter quietly stole the newspaper from James, knowing that once James got started, he seldom stopped talking. The three men were still in this configuration when the food was being placed in front of them by the bald waiter.

After thanking the waiter, they began to eat ravenously. The Florida East Coast Railway was known for its excellent food, and this breakfast had been no exception, with the particularly delightful blueberry muffins, although James did think that Maude's eggs were better.

As the clinking of silverware and the cacophony of voices filled the small space of the dining car, James looked up from his plate and his eyes caught Walter staring out of the window of the dining car. James turned his head to see what caught Walter's eyes. About twenty feet away stood a tall thin woman in a tan cloche hat with wisps of dark brown hair pushing out. As she walked towards the window, he immediately began to notice her eyes. He looked at Walter whose eyebrows were raised in appreciation at the beauty of the young woman. James turned once again and stared into her eyes, noticing the deep pools of brown flecked with green that gave them a hazel-like quality. He tore himself away and interrupted Walter's reverie.

"Walter, what are you staring at?" James said jokingly.

"Nothing, nothing," Walter responded but without any conviction.

"Uh-huh," James said. "I've seen that look on your face many times before. And every time is right before you go trying to neck somebody."

"I am not that bad!" Walter exclaimed.

Hugh chimed in, chuckling, "If I may add my two cents in, you do seem to have a propensity for knowing your onions when it comes to women."

Walter shot back, looking at James, "I'm not the only one who's been on the prowl on one of these trips."

"That was eleven years ago!" James argued. "And I married that one. Plus that was one trip. You are on the prowl on every trip!"

"Touche," Walter answered. "Well I'm allowed to look, aren't I?"

James shrugged his shoulders and thought to himself that she was beautiful. As Walter looked out the window again, James turned around to look as well.

She was gone.

AFTER BREAKFAST, JAMES excused himself and decided to walk down the train to have a smoke before going back to his compartment for the eight hour train ride from Jacksonville to Miami. He knew the speech needed much more work before Monday, but he needed to relax and avoid thinking about the speech and all it means for his future.

James walked into a passenger car and began to people watch as he walked down the aisle and the train began to move. The jolt bumped him into a seat, causing him to scrap his knees on a wooden hand rest. Cursing to himself, he looked around at each of the padded benches but didn't recognize anyone he knew. James hobbled down the aisle as he thought back on the conversation at breakfast, reminiscing of the history trip where he was on when he met Maude.

Knoxville, Tennessee - November 17, 1911 - James, a first-year professor, and Walter, his mentor, were attending a conference on southern history at the University of Tennessee. In the midst of this conference was a reception for the historians at Knollwood that had once served as General Longstreet's headquarters during the War Between the States. As the Tennessee whiskey was flowing, the bespeckled James was enjoying a dance with a young debutante when another woman in a long black skirt came over and asked to break in. James, feeling the effects of the whiskey, did not mind and soon was twirling around the room with this gregarious, outsized personality of a woman.

"I'm Maude Sparks!" the girl said energetically introducing herself to James as they began to sway around the dance floor.

"James Pashen," he responded cheekily.

Maude glowed as she asked, "So what is a young man like you doing at conference full of old men?"

"Well..." he said with a smart-alecky tone, "I teach southern history and this is a southern history conference."

"Well I figured that, silly. I just don't remember seeing men your age at these things."

James contemplated her statement before responding, "Well what is a young woman like you doing at this 'old man' party?"

She smiled a winning smile. "Father requested I come with him to help balance out the numbers."

"I need to remember to thank him sometime," James said staring into her eyes.

From across the room, Walter had his arm around a rock of ages and was whispering something in her ear when he looked at James. Walter knew James was terrible at hiding his emotions, which was why he always won money off James at cards. He noticed the look on his face and knew James was smitten. Walter whispered to the woman on his arm, "See my friend over there. I'd bet a necking session that boy doesn't leave that girl's side the rest of the night."

The older woman smiled. "No way I bet that, but I'll give you the session for free."

Walter chuckled before giving her his hand and leaving the room.

And Walter was right, James did not leave her side the rest of the night.

James was jolted out of his memory when he bumped into a young woman trying to pass him in the passenger car.

"Pardon me," the woman said as she looked into his eyes.

James immediately recognized her as the woman Walter had been staring at. He smiled, saying, "I was wool-gathering. Please pardon me."

She walked past and moved down the aisle of the train. James watched her walk away before turning and heading for the observation car.

James strolled into the observation car and found an opulent chair that happened to be empty. He grabbed his pipe from his jacket pocket and packed it with Lucky Strike tobacco. He began to stare out the car toward the ocean and trees that were flying by the window as he slowly puffed on the pipe.

James placed his elbows on his knees and asked himself quietly, "What do I do next?"

Taking a deep drag from the lip and swishing the smoke in his mouth, he knew that he had no answers. At 38, he had reached the pinnacle of his profession. To be the keynote speaker at the American Historians Association was an honor few had bestowed upon them. He had gained a full professorship at 31, and had published two books. He had a wonderful wife and smart children. He knew that everything was perfect on the outside. But where did he go from here?

Staring at the passing scenery, he took another deep drag on the pipe before putting it out. He exhaled and began to look around the observation car once again. He admired the wood paneling of the car that accentuated the dark furniture nicely. Sitting back, he began to eavesdrop on the conversation between two businessmen discussing their trip to Daytona Beach.

James silently thanked God that he did not live the traveling salesman life before getting up and walking down the observation car and back through the train. Encountering no one he knew, James made it to his compartment on the train. He pulled out the pages of his speech and began to edit it for the fourth time. He kept sensing the speech was lacking something, and he hoped beyond hope that he could get this speech right. Although he never thought of himself as ambitious from the standpoint of wanting a new position, being respected in the academic community was a lifelong goal, and here was his chance to obtain that respect. This speech was the most important of his career, but all that plagued his mind was what comes after the speech.

Chapter 2
The Driver

JAMES WAS UNABLE TO concentrate on editing the speech. Although he continued to stare at the words, his mind kept wandering back to his future. He placed the speech in his briefcase then closed his eyes. The motion of the train slowly lulled him into a deep sleep.

Several hours later, he groggily felt the train stop and opened his eyes to look out of the window. The sign on the station read "Hollywood, Florida." Knowing that this was the last stop before Miami, James got up, stretched his legs, and headed down the train to the dining car to get a drink.

Opening the door from his compartment, James began to walk down the train. Pipe in hand, he casually walked into the dining car. He walked down the aisle looking for an empty table when he noticed Walter's bushy gray eyebrows. James pulled the chair out and sat down across from him.

"James, my boy!" Walter exclaimed, puffing on a cigar.

"Yes, sir?"

"Where have you been keeping yourself today?" Walter wondered out loud. "We had a lively discussion with some colleagues from the University of Chicago. You know Ira Grossman?"

"By reputation only, he's the one who studies ancient Rome, right?"

"Yes," Walter responded. "He wrote that famous book about the Jewish contributions to ancient Rome. Anyway, you remember the pretty girl I saw at breakfast?"

James chuckled, "Yeah, I bumped into her in a passenger car after breakfast."

"Well, she is a protege of Ira's and she's smart as a whip!"

James peered over his glasses, frowning at Walter. "Don't get any ideas, Walter! I remember the co-ed from Mary Baldwin when I first came to Charlottesville."

Defending himself, Walter shot back, "That was 13 years ago, and I was much younger then. She's a pretty face and a brilliant mind, but she's not my type."

James rolled his eyes, "She's beautiful and smart, Walter. She's exactly your type."

"Let's just say, I have other plans for Miami."

"I'll believe it when I see it," James quipped. "So if she's not your type, what did you all discuss?"

"Mostly religion's influence on modern America, especially concerning the urban and rural differences," Walter noted. "Anyway, I think they are going to join us for a late dinner tonight if you want to come along."

"Of course, Walter," James said. "Maude wouldn't want me to reject any invitations of yours. She wanted me to mention to you that she still misses you coming over for dinner."

Walter and Maude had always gotten along like siblings. "So do you remember the time the three of us traveled to Richmond for that symposium on Jefferson Davis?" Walter asked chuckling to himself.

James rolled his eyes, "Yes, I do. I thought she was going to hit that woman who tried to talk to me."

Walter howled, "So did I! Maude is such a bearcat!"

"She's definitely something," James chuckled.

"She still jealous of Varina Davis?"

"I wouldn't say jealous, but she definitely is glad she's long dead," James joked.

The men looked out the window in companionable silence as the last of the people on the platform stepped slowly onto the train.

Walter looked back to James and asked, "So how much farther to Miami?"

"Shouldn't take but about 45 minutes once the train gets moving again," James noted.

A waiter dropped off two menus while walking past the table. Walter practically shouted as he looked over the menu. "Damn this Prohibition! I want a real drink."

"What happened to the flask you always carried? I had assumed you would have been one of the guys to get a rabbi's license," James cracked.

"You know I'm not Jewish!"

"Well, Ramsey is now a rabbi and his family has been Episcopal since the 1700s!"

"I haven't seen him in years, but maybe I'll send him a letter when I'm back in Boston," Walter joked as the waiter walked up.

After Walter ordered a tea and James a soda, the men noticed the low sun as the train pulled away from Hollywood on the way to Miami. Each stared at the orange sun glowing behind the lush green palm trees as the train sped toward Miami.

The waiter placed the drinks on the table, interrupting their peaceful silence. Brought back to reality, James asked Walter, "So tell me about Harvard?" which launched Walter into an excited soliloquy on Boston and his latest research on the Adams family. Walter then began to talk about the women of Boston and his latest conquests. James absorbed the information and Walter's enthusiasm, which made him realize that Walter was never coming back to Virginia. For some reason this gave James a deep sense of sadness that he would only see his mentor and closest friend during conferences and events.

Sipping their drinks, the men continued discussing Walter's love life before venturing into a discussion about Maude and the kids until a porter came walking through the car, his voice booming, "15 minutes until Miami! 15 minutes until Miami!"

James and Walter gulped down their drinks. Leaving the table, James asked, "Want to share a ride to the Flamingo?"

"Of course, son! Can Hugh join us?"

"Sounds good to me!" James said before turning and walking away from Walter and out of the dining car. James puffed on his pipe as he walked down the corridor, looking at everything and nothing until he got back to his compartment.

JAMES LET THE SMOKE casually escape his mouth as the brakes on the cars squeaked the train to a stop. Putting out his pipe, James grabbed his black suitcase and stepped out into the hall. He began to head for the closest exit toward the platform. He figured he would meet Walter and Hugh at the cabbie stand that was supposed to be outside the small white station that served as the end of the line for the Florida East Coast Railroad.

He dropped his luggage beside him as he waited for the line to move. As the freshly applied perfume of the woman in front of him flooded his senses, James stopped in front of a window. He grasped his gold watch from his pocket and glanced at the time before looking out to the platform.

Standing outside the window was Dr. Grossman's protege wearing the same tan clothe hat she had on in Jacksonville. She was immaculate with her brown hair curled around her cheek, her bright red lips tight as she concentrated on what she was looking for, and her neck tapering into slender shoulders that held a beautiful beige knee-length jacket that went straight down her body. James stared at her for a moment, appreciating her beauty before she looked into the window and saw him staring. He quickly darted his eyes away and looked back at his watch. He looked back up to see that she had walked on.

James quickly grabbed his suitcase and hurried down the corridor and out into the fresh salt air of Miami. Once outside the train car James's eyes were blinded by the luminescent Miami sun. He blindly followed the throng of people down the platform and towards the cabbie stand.

He walked slowly with the crowd through a series of white columns towards the front of the station. As he made it to the front of the throng of people, James spotted Walter and Hugh already at the cabbie stand as he walked over. He placed his suitcase down at his side and took off his brown fedora, which covered his salt and pepper hair. James exhaled heavily, which Walter noticed and frowned. He had worked with James for many years and knew his moods. So Walter decided to pull James aside as they waited for a cab to take them across the bay to the Flamingo Hotel on Miami Beach. After leaning over to Hugh to let him know what he was doing, Walter moved over to James.

"James..." Walter said concerned.

"What?" James spat, knowing what was coming next.

"You're still thinking about the speech and what it means for your life."

"So what if I am?"

"James, as your friend, let me remind you once again that you have a great job and a loving family. If you don't want this speech to mean anything more than one speech, it doesn't have to," Walter implored.

Exasperated, James replied while staring towards the sunset, "Walter, don't worry about it. I'm sure that the speech will go fine and I'll go back to Charlottesville and find a new goal."

Both men stood silent for a moment before Walter inquired, "What is this focus on the future about anyway?"

James focused on the sunset once again before looking to the clouds above. He ran his hand through his hair.

"I'm just in a rut right now." James said honestly.

"Well, snap out of it! We are hear to have a fun week in Miami!" Walter said, putting his arm around James's shoulders.

"You're right," James finally said, putting his fedora back on. "You're right. No more worrying about what is to come. Let's enjoy this week."

Walter looked relieved and said, "Let's grab that cab," as Walter noticed Hugh with his natural smirk on his face, waving frantically to get their attention. They walked over and got into a 4-door Yellow Cab. Hugh and Walter stepped onto the rail and entered the back seat which left James stuck next to the driver. James's natural reticence with new people quickly showed as he pushed his hat down and turned toward the window. He looked towards the city outside and was enraptured.

The bustling scenes of economic activity were everywhere. Just twenty years earlier, less than 6,000 people lived in Miami, but the city James noticed had upwards of 50,000 people. Buildings were springing up everywhere, with as many under construction as were occupied. Cars were dominating the new roads, so many being constructed that not all of them were paved yet. Miami was the very definition of a boom town.

James's ruminations were cut short by the southern twangy voice of the cabbie next to him. "So what brings you men to Miami?"

James, ever polite, turned to the driver, "We are here for the annual meeting of the American Historians Association."

"Historians, huh? Does that mean you are writers?" The cabbie asked.

"Sometimes," Hugh chuckled with that smirk on his face. "We are all professors at universities."

"Universities, huh," the cabbie grinned. "We could use some smart men like you down here leading this development. I'm telling you this land boom will bust sooner or later. Mark my words."

Hugh, ever the optimist, replied, "I'm sure you're wrong. Besides we are historians, not economists."

"Or city planners," Walter added.

"Well we will see, won't we?" The cabbie huffed before changing the subject, "So tell me men, what else do you plan to do in Miami besides go to the conference?"

"What do you recommend?" Piped up James, becoming interested in the cabbie's view of his city.

"Well, obviously the beach but you will already be there. If you enjoy modern architecture, there are several new buildings everywhere, and I may be bragging but the city has the best gin joints on the East Coast." The cabbie smiled proudly.

Never one to turn down talking about drinking, Walter interjected, "So how can Miami speakeasies compare to New York?"

"Cuban rum," was all the cabbie needed to say.

Walter was practically salivating as he said, "It's been a few years since I had a good Bacardi."

"Well you are in the right city to have some," the cabbie responded.

Walter continued, "So where would you recommend us going to find some of this Cuban rum?"

The cabbie smiled and said, "Well, you're in luck because the Flamingo has one of the best bars in the country. Another fine place is a bit harder to find but they have the best rum in Florida. It's name is Tobacco Road and you'll find it at South Miami Avenue. However, any good cabbie knows exactly where it is."

Walter thanked the man, before James asked politely, "So what's your name?"

"Samuel," the cabbie responded. "And what about you all?"

James answered pointing to the back seat, "My name is James, and my colleagues are Walter and Hugh."

"Nice to meet you, Mr. James, Mr. Walter, Mr. Hugh," the cabbie said respectfully.

Walter piped back in, "So if you could give us one piece of advice to enjoy the city this week, what would it be?"

"Enjoy the gin joints and the beautiful women, but don't get attached here," Samuel warned. "Miami has a way of wilting one's inhibitions and moralities. Enjoy the next few days, but be careful."

The men looked at each other as the car sped across the causeway towards Miami Beach. Hugh's smirk appeared before they all began to chuckle. Samuel just kept driving.

Chapter 3
The Hotel

JAMES STARED AT THE Flamingo Hotel as the cab pulled into the driveway for the hotel. He looked up and down the tall cream building that reflected the orangish tinge of the sunset. Staring at the palm trees that lined the driveway, he smiled approvingly when Samuel noticed James's look. "This is the fanciest hotel in the entire area," Samuel smiled. "Anytime I have passengers who stay here, they rave about this place. I hear the beds are particularly comfortable."

"Well, hopefully we will have a good few days," was James's only reply as he once again took in the concrete edifice with a gold dome on the top. The cab pulled to a stop, and bellhops began to descend upon the car, grabbing anything that did not seem to be tied down. As the men began to get themselves out of the vehicle, Walter grabbed some cash and paid the cabbie, saying, "Well that was quite enlightening! Thanks for the recommendations for entertainment."

"Don't forget my warning!" Samuel stated. "If the stars align, I will be your driver again this week."

"Thanks for the ride," James called out as Samuel began to drive away. The men turned and looked at each other. Walter's bushy eyebrows were raised as James rolled his eyes. "Well that was an educational experience!" Hugh said laughing. The guys walked toward the lobby, following the bellhops who were carrying their luggage.

James was pulling up the rear of the parade of men as they entered the lobby. He stopped and ogled the architecture around the lobby. Unlike most of the fancy hotels at which James had stayed during other conferences, the lobby floor of the Flamingo was covered with Spanish tile. Octagonal columns decorated the lobby and separated the different seating sections. The leather furniture and the plants around the lobby gave a sense of comfortable opulence. However, he was most interested in the beautiful Central American influenced decorations and began to try to count the number of flamingos in the sculptures, in the murals, and even on the tables. There were flamingos everywhere. James mused quietly to himself, "This is what Havana must be like."

As James was taking in the beauty of the lobby, an older gentleman with a cane that clanked on the tile with every step came up to James. He proceeded to rap him in the back of the head. "James, James! Pay attention, son! You'll miss things!"

James rubbed the back of his head. "Ow! What are you doing?" James asked frustratedly.

"Saying hello, son!" The old man responded sardonically.

The men stared down each other before both smiled and the old man pulled James into a huge hug.

After hugging him, the old man put his hands on James's shoulders. "I'm so glad to see you, son."

"Dr. Abney, It's an honor to see you again." James said to his former professor from college. George Pickett Abney, although only 59, had a baseball injury from his youth and had been using a cane since he was 30. Named after the Confederate General, Dr. George Pickett Abney had taught James at Alabama Polytechnic Institute before James had gone on to graduate school at Vanderbilt. James was Abney's prize student and the only one he ever taught who became a professor of history as well. Abney loved him.

"I saw on the schedule that you will be speaking on Monday," Abney noted.

"Yes, sir."

"I'm proud of you, son, but please don't tell me it's on the poor people of the South again! I'm tired of you focusing on them. Use your immense talents to write the great book on Bob Lee or Jeff Davis," Abney pleaded.

James grimaced and rolled his eyes, having received this advice regularly for the past eighteen years. In fact, James could not remember the last time he ran into Dr. Abney in which this topic did not come up. "Dr. Abney, you know that my interests have always been in relation to the average people. Besides, if I'm going to write the great southern biography, it would be about Varina Davis, not Jefferson."

Abney chuckled, "Of course, of course, I always forgot about your great crush on Varina Davis. Wasn't that what got Maude so riled up in Richmond all those years ago?"

"We try not to speak of that incident, sir," James said laughing with him..

Abney hit James on the arm with the cane before saying, "Well son, they have asked me to introduce you before your speech."

"I'm honored they asked you, sir."

Abney smiled. "I hope you'll make time to have a meal with me, if Dr. Shafer hasn't already monopolized all your time." Abney joked, knowing how close James and Walter were.

"I'll see what I can do to find some time, sir," James smiled. "I do agree that Walter can be a pretty demanding partner in crime."

James was about to try to arrange a lunch sometime after Monday's speech when a large man came lumbering up to Dr. Abney, "George, my old friend, how are you, sir?"

"I'm upright and taking nourishment," Abney responded sarcastically. "And you Ira?"

"As well as a Yankee Jew can be doing in the deep South!"

Both men laughed as they shook hands.

Dr. Abney performed the introductions. "Ira, I'd like for you to meet James Pashen. James, this is Ira Grossman, from the University of Chicago."

James, as the polite southern man always did, extended his hand to shake Ira's. Ira recognized the name. "James Pashen? Are you the protege of Walter Shafer?"

James blushed a bit, knowing that Abney also liked to claim that title. "Kind of. I worked with Walter for many years at the University of Virginia."

"Yes, yes, he mentioned you this afternoon when we ran into each other on the train. I'm looking forward to dinner this evening," Ira smiled.

"Dinner?" Abney perked up.

"Sorry Dr. Abney. I would invite you, but we plan to be going to a place you would disapprove of," James said, knowing Abney was a Southern Baptist and a teetotaler.

"Ah well," Dr. Abney sighed. He extended his hand to Ira, "Always good to see you Ira! And James, I'll find you for that meal later in the week."

"Yes, sir," James responded although he could already hear the clomp of the cane as Dr. Abney limped away.

"Well, Dr. Grossman, I believe it is time for me to check in," James said shaking Ira's hand once again.

Ira called out, "I'll see you in a bit," as James headed to the desk to check in.

JAMES WALKED DOWN THE dimly lit corridor that was lined with half columns between each door. He stared at each number, looking for room 316. As his black suitcase continued to thump against his leg, James began to plan the expected evening in his head. He looked at his watch to make sure he had the right time, but the dim hallway made the watch impossible to read. He wondered if that was on purpose.

He arrived at the door, inserted the key and turned the knob to enter room 316. A blast of light welcomed him as he squinted his eyes to get a better view of the room. In his line of sight, James noticed a bed directly across from the door, a chest of drawers to the left of the bed and a desk with a wooden chair on his right. James entered the room and placed his suitcase on top of the white blanket covering the bed. He walked to the window where the thin linen curtains were fluttering from a slight breeze outside. At this time of day in Virginia, he would have been hunched over the fireplace trying to warm up after a walk from campus back to the house. Here in south Florida, standing in the window wearing a light blue button down shirt, James thanked God for the beautiful winter weather of Miami Beach.

James heard shouting outside the window and looked down to see a fierce tennis match being played just over the palm trees below. As the two men smacked the ball back and forth, James took his pipe out and lit the tobacco. He put the bit in his mouth, becoming engrossed in the match. James leaned against the window frame and watched the match for several minutes. As his pipe got low, he looked at his watch and realized he had things to do before dinner.

James walked over to the suitcase and began to unload his items into the wooden chest of drawers that was opposite the double bed. Meticulously placing each item in a specific place, he finished unloading his clothing before placing his toiletries in the room's bath area.

Knowing that he may not have time again until after the speech on Monday, James walked over to the desk. He took out some stationary from the desk and grabbed his pen. Beginning the letter, *Dear Maude*, he began relating everything that had happened on the train that day. He wrote long paragraphs about Walter and seeing Dr. Abney. Finishing the letter talking about meeting

Ira Grossman, James placed the pen down and looked back outside as the sunlight was finally disappearing.

He read over the letter after finishing it. Looking up to the ceiling, he breathed in a deep breath. Maybe he should tell Maude about his concerns about his future. After all, he never hid anything from Maude.

James walked to the bathroom, deciding to leave the letter alone for a few minutes. He looked in the mirror, staring at himself. He whispered, "What should I do?" Knowing he should pray about it, but not wanting to hear the answer God might have, James contemplated whether Maude needed to know. After struggling with his conscience, he decided to leave the letter as is. There was no need for her to worry about his future right now.

James began to undress to take a shower before dinner, deciding that he could address the letter right before he went down to the lobby to meet the other historians and head to Tobacco Road. He stepped in the shower and rubbed his face under the water. He would deal with his future alone for now.

Chapter 4
The Speakeasy

JAMES LEFT HIS ROOM, the letter to Maude plastered to his right hand. Unable to relax because of his nervousness about Monday's speech, he carefully took the stairs as his blue suit pants scratched lightly with each step. Placing his fedora on his head as he entered the lobby, James was thankful that Tobacco Road was not a ritzy place, which allowed him to wear a regular suit instead of dinner attire.

He glanced around quickly for some of his party, but seeing no one he knew, James walked over to the desk to post his letter to Maude in Knoxville. The coins clinked together in his pocket as he grabbed a couple of them and handed them to the man at the desk. James thanked the attendant before walking to a part of the lobby where a small fountain was gurgling and a concrete bench stood ready. He sat down on the bench and leaned against the pillar behind him.

Closing his eyes, James tried to shut out the noise around him and focus on the speech for Monday. He hoped by visualizing it he could ease his nervousness. However, all James could seem to think about was that there was no where to go but down after the speech. He opened his eyes and leaned forward, staring into the water of the fountain. After a moment, the glint of a penny at the bottom of the fountain caught his eye. James took out a penny himself and tossed it into the fountain, making a silent wish as the coin began to flutter down.

James closed his eyes again saying a silent prayer when he heard the familiar voice of Walter bellowing to someone as footsteps got closer. James opened his eyes and stood as Walter, Hugh, Ira, and a couple of professors James didn't know walked up. After introductions were made, James, Walter and Ira began to become engrossed in a conversation on the impact of Jewish soldiers in the Civil War.

As more men walked up, Walter realized that he didn't see Ira's mentee.

"So what happened to your student?" Walter inquired to Ira, changing the topic abruptly.

Ira, having known Walter for many years, looked warily at him before answering, "She had to meet with Jeanette Fallon from Barnard College about some research she has been doing. They are both going to join us later."

"Oh really?" James asked, taking his hat off and flipping it in his hands. "What's she been working on?"

Ira exhaled, "She is fascinated with the early saints of the Catholic Church and Dr. Fallon is the preeminent historian in the country on the early church, so they are discussing this topic before joining us at Tobacco Road."

Walter and James both tried to speak at the same time. Deferring to his mentor, James quieted down as Walter inquired hopefully, "So is Dr. Fallon single?"

Ira laughed, "I should have known that would be your first question, Walter."

"Well?"

"Last I heard, she was still single."

Walter's eyebrows moved up and down in excitement. "Well, maybe this will be a good night after all!" He said slapping Ira on the back.

Ira rolled his eyes while smiling. "So, Dr. Pashen, you seemed to want to say something," Ira stated, turning his attention toward James.

"Well, I had noticed your expression when discussing your mentee's interests. Do you think her research a waste of her time?" James asked respectfully.

Ira looked at James alarmed before replying, "Please don't share that with her. I just think she is so talented and such a gifted historian, but she's focusing all her attention on the early Christian church rather than Ancient Rome at large."

James grinned. "You sound like Dr. Abney. He always wanted me to focus on the greats of the South, while I've always been more interested in the poor white trash and slaves."

"And how is that working out for you?"

"Well, I'm making the keynote speech here on Monday."

"Touche, Dr. Pashen, touche," Ira smiled.

At that point, Walter, who was ready to try some of the Cuban rum, called to the crowd of male historians that had gathered in the lobby, "Are we ready to find some cabs?"

TEN MINUTES LATER, James and Walter had climbed into the backseat of a Yellow Cab. Ira had volunteered to sit in the front seat, being much larger than the other two men. Samuel happened to be their driver again as the cab sped across the causeway to the mainland.

"So you've decided to take my advice and head to Tobacco Road?" Samuel asked already knowing the answer. "The password for the week is Havana, and ask to be seated in Florence's section. She'll take good care of you and she's a sight to look at."

James quickly jumped in. "I thought you warned us to not fall in love in Miami."

"I did. That doesn't mean you shouldn't enjoy the finest Miami has to offer. Just don't lose yourself to it," Samuel added.

"James, my boy, quit being a spoilsport. I, for one, am all for drinks and women!" Walter exclaimed.

Ira chuckled at his old friend, "Well, I'm always down for a good drink."

"That's the spirit!"

James chimed in, "So is it my turn to look out for you, Walter?"

"I have no reason to have to look out for anything. It's been many years since I had a woman to answer to at home."

Ira turned around from the front and asked Walter, "So will you be on the hunt?"

"Have you ever been with me when I wasn't on the hunt?" Walter responded.

"Well there was this one time...," Ira began as the cab slowed to a stop.

Samuel cut him off, stating, "Now remember boys, enjoy yourself but don't lose yourself in Tobacco Road. After all, every temptation under the sun will be under that roof. Now have fun! Don't forget to ask for Florence."

James and Walter exchanged a look and all but laughed. James took a dollar bill out of his wallet and handed it to Samuel. "Thanks again for the ride!"

The men stepped out of the cab and on to the electric-lit sidewalk. Breathing in the crisp Miami air, they walked toward the front door of the bakery. Although the sign said bakery outside, the only thing the men could smell as they walked through the door was stale tobacco smoke. A hunchbacked woman stood at the counter, taking a drag of a cigarette. "What can I get for you fine gentlemen this evening?"

"Well, we were looking for the way to Cuba?" Walter muttered in a way he thought was clever.

James rolled his eyes as he quickly said, "He is trying to say Havana."

"Why spoil my fun?"

"Because I want a drink now. It's been three days."

The hunched over woman broke in, "Boys, are you ready?"

"Yes," they all responded at once.

She began to shuffle over to a bookcase that was also a door. Pulling it open, she pointed up the stairs and said, "Now don't get into too much trouble, boys!" as the three men followed her gesture and walked into the tight stairwell. Grabbing hold of the wooden rail, James led the three men up the dark staircase and into the bar.

At the top of the stairs was a large man in a tuxedo sitting on a stool. Looking bored, he asked the men, "What can I do for you?"

Walter, realizing this was not a man to trifle with, responded respectfully, "We would like a table in Florence's section, please."

Barely moving, but continuing to stare at Walter, the large man motioned to a young woman in a very short black dress. He whispered in her ear before she approached Walter and asked, "Is it just you three?"

"No, we will have a party of about twelve when it's all said and done," Walter responded.

"Right this way," the young woman gestured, as the men followed her into the main part of the bar. As they walked into the area, the sounds of jazz wafted through the smoke-filled room. James glanced around and noticed a wooden bar set up on the right side of the room with a man in an open-collared shirt mixing some type of cocktail. Tables circled a small dance floor which was packed with nighttime revelers. A small jazz band was set up in the back left corner, playing a song James did not immediately recognize. Although small in size, the room had a cozy atmosphere and James was looking forward to a fun evening of drinking with colleagues.

As the woman showed them the three tables that would be theirs for the evening, she smiled and motioned back to them, "Florence will be right with you all!"

The three men sat down and began to listen to the band as they broke into an instrumental version of "Down Hearted Blues." The men glanced at each other before bursting into laughter. Walter joked as he lit up a cigar, "I bet Samuel the cab driver told the band to play that for us!"

James jumped in, imitating Samuel's deep southern accent, "Now you better be careful in Miami, or you may have some downhearted blues."

Ira, being the voice of reason, chastised James, "Samuel means well. Besides the fact that he didn't realize that women aren't what I'll be looking for tonight."

"What year was it when you convinced me to go to your type of bar? I think it was in New Haven?" Walter asked reminiscing.

"1922, and I'd say that was a productive night for me," Ira smiled remembering the night well.

"Yeah? Well all I did is get drunk because there wasn't any women in that dandy bar for me. Remind me James, why didn't you make that trip? You would have never dragged me to a dandy bar." Walter joked.

James entered the conversation, stating, "Paul was born during the week of the convention in 1922. Maude still doesn't like that I miss his birthday, but she understands that it's a part of my job."

"Well if she knew all the things we got up to at these conventions, she'd like it even less," Walter cracked.

"Walter, you know I tell her everything."

Walter blushed and looked worried, "Does everything include my escapades?"

"Well no. So not everything, but everything involving me, including the bars and parties and alcohol. Honestly, she's more envious than mad."

"That does sound like the Maude I know and love," Walter laughed.

Ira jumped back in the conversation, asking, "Will I ever get to meet this Maude?"

James, turning to Ira, said, "Only if you come to visit us in Charlottesville sometime."

"Charlottesville!" Hugh chimed in as he and a few others walked up to the table. "Haven't been there in years but always thought it was such a beautiful place!"

With his smirky smile on his face, Hugh extended his hand and James took it. The other men began to find seats as Florence walked over to the table. Her bright red hair cut into a bob, Florence wore a white tassel dress and had a cigarette tray hanging from her shoulder.

In a southern drawl, she began her spiel, "Welcome to Tobacco Road, I'm Florence and I'll be taking care of y'all this evening. We got a new shipment of Bacardi rum from Cuba just yesterday, so pretty much all our specials will include rum in them. Now most of the rum cocktails that you can get in the North we have here as well, but my recommendation is the Planter's Punch. The fresh citrus fruits we have in Florida make this a wonderful drink. So I'll start going around the tables and getting your drink orders."

James and Hugh started joking about how glad they were that the ministers from their Presbyterian churches did not know where they were tonight when Florence leaned over and asked, "Whatcha drinking, honey?" to James.

James turned and looked into her bright blue eyes and smiled, thinking that a little harmless flirting with this woman wouldn't hurt anything, especially if it would help get his troubles out of his mind. "So you recommend the Planter's Punch?"

"I do," she smiled touching his arm.

"Then I'll be happy to try it."

And then she moved on down the table. James leaned over to Hugh and whispered, "Well this night just got a little better."

JAMES TOOK ANOTHER sip of his Planter's Punch, savoring the fresh citrus taste. He asked, "So, Walter, who has IT tonight?"

Walter continued to look around the room before replying, "I think I'm going to wait and perhaps take a chance on Dr. Fallon."

"I don't think I've met her before."

"Well, I have met her a couple of times over the past year at different events. She keeps me on my toes."

"Keeps you on your toes?"

"Yeah, it's not often I get to be attracted to someone beautiful and intelligent."

James looked incredulous. "Could the great Walter Shafer actually be in love?"

"Now, now," Ira cut in. "I want a piece of this fun. You like Jeanette?" Ira boomed.

"Quiet down, I don't know when they will arrive," Walter pleaded.

"This is amazing! I can't wait to meet her."

Walter wanted to change the subject so he asked Ira, "So do you think there are any men in here that might be interested?"

Ira frowned slightly, "Well I've been watching the drummer of the band. Don't know if he'd like a father time like me but he's a possibility. That looks about it in here."

James, fascinated, asked, "So you can really tell if another man is a fairy?"

"Usually, yes. But I prefer finding queens."

"Queens?" James asked.

"Ah yes, you probably don't know the speak. The guys I like are generally more, how should I say this...girly."

James's eyes widened in comprehension as he finished his drink. "I think I'll go get another one. Anyone need a refill?"

Walter stood up and offered to go over to the bar with him. As they walked away from the table, Walter asked, "James, I need a favor."

"Sure. What is it?"

Walter looked around to make sure Ira wasn't nearby. "When the ladies get here, I need you to distract Ira's protege. I need some time to woo Dr. Fallon and I'm afraid the young woman Ira brought might be attached to Jeanette's hip all night."

James looked at Walter warily. "Walter, we haven't done the diversion thing in many years, plus what about Maude?"

Walter looked pleadingly. "I'm not asking you to middle aisle her. Just pay attention to her so I can have some time with Jeanette."

James took out his pipe and packed the tobacco in silence. After lighting the tobacco, he looked back at Walter. "I'll do this for you tonight, but you promise me that Maude hears nothing of it."

"Deal," Walter said putting his arm around James. "I really like this one."

"You better," James said.

As Walter walked back over to the table, James walked over to the bar. The band was playing an upbeat rendition of "Crazy Blues," as James eyed Florence near the bar and headed to talk to her. James was almost to the bar when he turned his head toward the staircase. Standing there were two women, the first he noticed was a short woman, perhaps in her mid-40s, wearing a creme-colored sleeveless dress. The second was Ira's protege. Stopping dead in his tracks, he watched her as she smoothed her black lace dress down, noticing a black headband around her dark brown hair. She slowly brought her cigarette holder to her mouth and inhaled. He stood mesmerized as she and the other woman talked with the big man on the stool. James realized that distracting this young woman this evening might turn out to be rather enjoyable. Forgetting to get another drink, James headed back to the table, ready to be introduced to the woman he was to distract for the next few hours.

Dr. Fallon and her companion weaved their way around the small dance floor and over to where the table full of men were sitting. James barely gave Dr. Fallon a second glance as she sat down next to Walter. Instead, he continued to stare avidly at the young woman from the platform, who was walking around the side of the table and took a seat two chairs away from James, next to Ira. If he had not already had a few drinks, he would not have been as obvious. However, all James could do was drink in her appearance, entranced by her eyes and her smile as Ira introduced her to those around the table. James was even smitten as she genuinely looked interested in each person at the table, asking them questions, and engaging with them.

As James was on Ira's right, he was the last one she was introduced to.

"James," Ira said. "This is Julia O'Connor, she is a student of mine at the University of Chicago. Julia, this is James Pashen, a professor of southern history at the University of Virginia."

James extended his hand to shake hers and as she reached out and touched him, he looked into her eyes and some type of energy passed through him.

He smiled to himself and thought, *Thank you, Walter. I owe you one.*

Chapter 5
The Dance

AFTER THE INTRODUCTION, James was about to engage Julia in conversation when someone else asked her a question and she turned to that man instead. James instead looked over to Walter who was already engaged in some debate with Dr. Fallon, and James realized that he may not need to talk to Julia after all. Walter was already making his move and Julia was sufficiently distracted for the time being. So James downed his drink before deciding there was no harm in appreciating Julia's beauty. Pipe in hand, he furtively stared at her eyes as much as he could get away with.

Florence walked back over to the table, checking on everyone and taking refill orders when she got to James. Kneeling down next him, she tried to get his attention, saying, "Would you like a refill?"

He tore his eyes away from Julia to smile at Florence. "I'd love another Planter's Punch!"

She smiled and put her hand on his leg, "I thought earlier you were looking at me like you wanted to get to know me better, but now I see I no longer have your attention."

James chuckled, "Yeah, my friend here," motioning toward Walter with his head, "needed me to help him out by distracting the other woman, so I've been watching her to see if I need to step in."

"Really? Because you sure seem to be enjoying looking at her."

James looked surprised when Florence added, "Don't worry. Your secret is safe with me." She patted his knee three time before standing up and saying, "I'll go get that punch now."

"Thanks!" James responded as he contemplated Florence's insight.

He sat back and pulled on the pipe once again, letting the smoke waft out of his mouth as he realized that Florence was right, he did find Julia striking, especially her eyes. As Florence returned with another punch, James thanked her for it and began to drink deeply. Noticing that Julia was ending her conversation and trying to get Dr. Fallon's attention, James knew it was time to horn in on the conversation.

James leaned closer to Ira and said, "Can we switch seats for a few minutes? I want to ask Miss O'Connor a question."

"Sure, Dr. Pashen. This will give me an opportunity to see if Florence can help me get an introduction to the drummer."

James laughed and patted Ira on the back before shifting over into the large, genial professor's chair. He immediately leaned over near Julia to ask her a question when he noticed the simple diamond ring adorning her right ring finger. Hesitating for just a second, he leaned back and took a gulp of his Planter's Punch before deciding that he wasn't hitting on her, he was only distracting her from Dr. Fallon.

"Excuse me, Miss O'Connor, but Dr. Grossman was mentioning your interest in the early Christian Church," James asked, hoping it would get her talking.

Julia turned slowly toward James and smiled a bit warily, "Yes, Dr. ... I'm sorry I forgot your name."

"Dr. Pashen, but please feel free to call me James."

"Well, James, I am fascinated by the early Catholic Church, but especially the idea of saints and their backgrounds," Julia answered before taking a sip of her drink. She continued, "My specific research right now is on my patron, Catherine of Alexandria."

"Well, since I'm not Catholic, can you tell me about her, and what you're looking for?" James asked hopefully.

Julia stared at him for a moment, unsure why James had any interest in this topic, but decided if he asked, she was going to tell him because she loved talking about the saints, and few people gave her a chance to do so.

And so began their conversation, as Julia described the life of Catherine of Alexandria. She elaborated on patron saints, why she had chosen Catherine, and what documents she was looking for to continue her research. James was riveted. He listened intently while smiling at the right times and staring into her eyes more than he should.

"So now, let me get this all straight," James contemplated as he took another sip of Planter's Punch. "This Catherine died on a wheel?"

"Yes, it was rather gruesome," Julia responded, pulling out a Lucky Strike cigarette and placing it in her black holder. James extended his arm and flicked his lighter for her.

"Did most saints die this way?"

"On a wheel or just gruesome?"

"Oh just gruesome. I would assume a wheel of death would be rather unique," James laughed.

"Yes, many lost their lives rather violently. How, as a historian, do you not know this?" She joked charmingly.

"Well early Catholic history is not exactly my speciality," James responded, finishing up his latest drink and beginning to feel uninhibited.

"Well then, Dr. Pashen, what is your specialty?"

"Social History in the Antebellum South."

"So what? You write about rich people history?" Julia smirked, her eyes dancing with delight.

James burst into laughter. "I've never had someone put it quite like that."

"Well isn't that the history of the Old South?"

"Well, it's a little bit more nuanced than that," James said. Noticing Julia's drink was getting low, he asked her, "Can I get you another drink?"

"Sure, I'd like another Mary Pickford."

Julia handed James her glass as he stood to walk to the bar. When James had crossed the room and got to the bar, Ira was there and looked agitated. Ira immediately chimed in.

"Dr. Pashen, I don't like this."

"I'm sorry, Dr. Grossman, but what are you talking about?" James asked, playing dumb.

"Dr. Pashen, Miss O'Connor is like the daughter I never had. She is engaged to be married and you are married. There is nothing good that can come from you paying attention to her."

Walter, having noticed the conversation, walked up and joined them.

"What's going on here, boys! I want my share of the fun."

Ira turned on Walter, "Did you know about this...this... this attention Dr. Pashen is paying to Julia?"

Walter sheepishly answered, "Maybe."

Ira roared back at James, "You will stay away from her!"

Walter stepped in, "Ira, will you let me explain everything to you?"

Ira looked warily at Walter and then James. "I want to hear it from Dr. Pashen."

"Ira," Walter said calmly, "He is doing it for me. Let me explain."

The men began to talk quietly as James grabbed two drinks and headed back to the table. As he handed Julia her drink and sat back down next to her, James changed the subject from Catholic saints to the event at hand. "So, Miss O'Connor, how did you end up in Miami with a bunch of old professors?"

"Well, Dr. Grossman thought that it was important for me to start making connections for the future, as I will be heading to graduate school next year, hopefully at Barnard," Julia said as she took a sip of her Mary Pickford.

"Oh, so you hope to study under Dr. Fallon?" James asked as he looked over at Walter and Dr. Fallon in deep conversation. James smiled realizing his diversion was working for Walter.

"Yes, although that would mean moving to New York."

"And what about your fiance, what does he do?" James asked casually.

"Well Albert is a student at the University of Chicago like I am. He's hoping to find a job in whatever city I end up for grad school."

"That's good. What's his focus of study?"

"Chemistry," Julia responded.

"Smarter than me then," James joked.

"Not smarter necessarily, just a different kind of smart," Julia said, drinking more and beginning to look a bit bent.

Dr. Fallon called across the table at Julia asking her to go to the powder room with her. James took this opportunity to go refill his drink and Walter noticed and followed him to the bar.

As they arrive at the bar, Walter bought them both shots of whiskey which they downed in one before both leaning on the bar and looking towards the dance floor. "So how is the night going, Walter?" James asked.

Walter smiled big. "I really think she might like me. This is the third time we've been at a convention together and each time she seems more and more open to me."

James patted him on the back, smiling, "Walter, that's wonderful. Maude would be so happy to hear that you might actually settle down."

"Let's not put the cart before the horse. We haven't even petted yet, but I do hope that will change soon." Walter ordered two punches before asking, "So how is the Julia assignment going?"

"So far so good. Doesn't hurt that she's charming and a sight to look at."

Walter looked worried, "Now don't overdo it. I just need you to distract her, not to carry a torch for her."

"Walter, I'm fine, I'm just half under."

Walter looked across the room and saw the two women again, and said, "Alright then, if you're ok, it's time for you to go back to work."

James smiled and walked away from Walter, heading directly to Julia, before asking her, "Would you like to dance?"

AS THE BAND PLAYED a slow rendition of Irving Berlin's "All by Myself," James's right hand felt the black lace of Julia's dress. They moved slowly around the dance floor, swaying together to the music. He tried but failed to wipe the drunk grin off his face as their cheeks nearly touched during the slow waltz.

After about two minutes of this, she pulled her head back slightly to look into his eyes since they were nearly the same height. "So tell me, Dr. Pashen, why is a married man dancing with a college student in some dark speakeasy at the end of the world?"

James pondered her question for a moment, looking around the room, "So do you want me to impress you or tell you the truth?"

Julia replied charmingly, "Are they different answers?"

James chuckled, "Not necessarily."

They moved slowly in silence for a moment before Julia spoke again, "Well how about you tell me the impressive truth."

"Miss O'Connor, do you really not realize that truth yet?"

She rolled her eyes. "Realize what, Dr. Pashen?"

"You are the most beautiful woman in this room," James said staring into her eyes. "How could I not ask the most beautiful woman in the room to dance?"

She moved her head back next to his as they continued to dance. As the song ended, James asked, "Please may I have another dance?"

Flattered from earlier, Julia responded, "How can I say no to such a plea?"

James smiled and Julia quickly added, "But you have to tell me, what made you come to believe I was the most beautiful woman in the room?"

James stiffened slightly and Julia noticed his shoulders tense up which made her laugh.

"Oh so there must be a good story there. Let me guess. You saw me walking in this short dress and you couldn't take your eyes off my gams," Julia ribbed.

James shook his head. His hand pressed against her lower back."No. That wasn't it."

"Hmmm," she mumbled as she smiled and looked at him again. "Then it must have been when I smiled as Dr. Grossman introduced you earlier."

"You'll never guess it," James said as he lightly guided her around the dance floor.

Julia looked incredulous. "Now part of our deal to keep dancing was you'd tell me why you thought I was the most beautiful woman in the room."

"What if I told you that I thought of your beauty long before this speakeasy?" James revealed, smirking slightly as his blue eyes widened.

"I'd call you a liar," Julia joked.

"I saw your eyes this morning."

"Where?"

"You were on the platform in Jacksonville. I saw you from the dining car," James admitted.

"Really? And what did you think?"

James looked directly into her brown eyes and said, "That you have the most beautiful eyes I've ever seen."

Julia rolled her eyes, "And that's it?"

As the dim lights of the dance floor shone on James's salt and pepper hair, he responded, "Well at first I was enamored with the shape of them, but then when the early morning sunlight reflected on the hazel flecks, they seemed to come alive." James said with a slightly slurred speech. Throwing caution to the wind, he added, "I will never forget that moment. I was mesmerized by your eyes."

Part II
Sunday, January 6, 1924

Chapter 6
The Church

JAMES WOKE WITH A START.

Still disoriented from the copious amounts of alcohol he had consumed, he glanced back and forth around the strange hotel room. He drunkenly stumbled to the bathroom and turned on the light. He looked back to the bed and the clock next to it read 3:16. Frustrated he was awake; James filled up a cup with water and took a few sips. He stared into his own eyes in the mirror in front of him, reminiscing about the few hours before.

Miami, Florida - January 5, 1924 - "That you have the most beautiful eyes I've ever seen."

Julia rolled her eyes, "And that's it?"

As the dim lights of the dance floor shone on James's salt and pepper hair, he responded, "Well at first I was enamored with the shape of them, but then when the early morning sunlight reflected on the hazel flecks, they seemed to come alive. I will never forget that moment. I was mesmerized by your eyes."

Julia blushed at James's compliment as she placed her cheek next to his. James smiled knowing that what he had said affected her at least a little. Both a little nervous now, neither said anything else during the rest of the song. As the song ended, James asked Julia, "Would you like another drink?"

Julia smiled and said, "Sure."

He extended his arm, and she placed her hand on his elbow. They walked slowly to the bar, almost leaning on each other. After ordering drinks, James and Julia began to speak quietly to each other about her conversation with Dr. Fallon earlier. A minute later, the bartender came back with the drinks and James handed him a couple of dollars.

After each taking a long sip of their drinks, James pulled out his pipe while Julia placed a cigarette in her black and gold holder. James lit both of them before inquiring, "So tomorrow is January 6, which is Epiphany. Is that a big deal in the Catholic Church?"

Julia looked at him curiously, "Why are you asking about Epiphany?"

"Just had a thought about the date, and the fact that I know so little of Catholic traditions."

"Well, the nativity scene will finally be finished with the adding of the Magi, as well as this marking the end of the Christmas season," Julia mentioned as she took a drag off her cigarette. "I hope I can find a place to go to Mass tomorrow."

"After a night like this?"

Julia laughed, lightly moving her hand on the edge of the bar. "Especially after a night like this."

They stood in silence, each finishing their smoke before James offered to walk her back to their table. Again he gave his arm to Julia to escort her. James purposefully walked slowly hoping to feel her hand on his elbow for another minute.

When they were back at the table, there was not a place to sit next to her, so James took a seat halfway down the table from Julia, and tried not to look too forlorn as he was unable to speak to her again the rest of the night.

James rubbed his eyes and looked in the mirror. What must this girl think of him? He unabashedly flirted with her for over an hour. Now he understood why she felt the need to go to church in the morning. Shaking his head at his own behavior, he headed back to the bed. As he came to the alarm clock, he stared at it for a moment. He grabbed it and looked at the time and decided on the spur of the moment to set the alarm for 8:00. He hoped that would give him enough time.

He was out as soon as his head hit the pillow.

BBRRRRIINNNNGG!!

James's head shot up from the pillow, not remembering that he had set the alarm for 8:00. Startled for a moment, he sat still on the bed as he began to remember that he woke up in the middle of the night and set the alarm to get ready for church. He shook his head in disgust, wondering what he was thinking. Just because he might have offended her by flirting didn't mean he had to follow her to church to apologize.

James continued to ponder the situation for several minutes, but when he realized he had no better ideas, he stood up and headed to the bathroom to get himself cleaned up to get a taxi into the city and hopefully choose the right Catholic Church.

After a shower and a shave, James flipped through the suits in his closet before deciding on the brown cashmere suit with a blue polka-dot bowtie. Glancing in the mirror one more time, he felt satisfied with how he looked and was ready to head downstairs. James grabbed his hat and left the room.

James walked into the dining room of the hotel, intent on grabbing breakfast before heading out to find a taxi. White dining cloths covered the rounded tables, while bow-tied waiters darted from table to table filling up waters and taking breakfast orders. He noticed Walter sitting at a table by himself, and decided to join him. As he sat down, James breathed in the aroma of freshly fried bacon from the table next to them. After ordering a fruit cocktail and some rolls with butter, Walter looked up from his newspaper and smiled as he said, "Now James, I've never seen you up this early after a night of drinking."

"Well, I wanted to get a fresh start on the day. I do have a big speech tomorrow after all."

Walter's bushy eyebrows raised in disbelief. "If you're up this early because of that speech then I'm Rudolph Valentino. You're up because of the girl."

"Don't be silly, Walter."

"Then tell me why you are dressed up, because I know you well enough to know you never go to church when you are on the road."

"Actually Walter, that is exactly where I am heading this morning."

Walter looked skeptical, so he pressed further, "So where is the Presbyterian Church you're going to attend this morning? You know it's not my normal thing, but I'd be glad to keep you company."

James, startled by the suggestion, said nothing for a moment, taking a sip of water instead. Walter quickly caught on and asked, "So what type of church are you actually planning to attend today?"

James blushed but decided to answer honestly, "I thought I might try a Catholic Church this morning."

"Catholic, huh. That wouldn't be because of a certain Miss O'Connor, would it?" Walter jabbed, chuckling.

"Perhaps," James answered sheepishly.

"I knew it! You do know the night is over, right?" Walter said with a slight bite in his voice.

James rolled his eyes. "I know that Walter but I flirted too much last night and feel the need to apologize. So here I am."

"Well then, do you know where to look?"

James shook his head. "I don't, but I'm hoping I can either spot her or find out from someone where the local Catholic Church is."

"Well good luck finding her. I never got to talk to you after the dance."

"Well let's just say we seemed to get a little too close, but I'm sure that was just the alcohol talking," James explained.

"Let's hope so," Walter said. "Of course, I've never seen you pay that much attention to a Jane since the night you met Maude."

"Walter, I did that last night for you."

"You didn't look like you minded."

James shrugged. "She was witty, sarcastic, bright. She was a fun date, but it was only one night."

Walter smiled and said, "Sounds like you had a good night. Just don't forget about Maude."

James looked down before looking at Walter and saying, "I don't think you have to worry about it. As much as I was enjoying the evening, it was one night where I got ossified and realized I got a little too close to her. Speaking of getting too close, what about you and Dr. Fallon?"

Walter delayed this time before answering, "I enjoyed our conversation but nothing else happened last night."

"But do you think the bank is closed?"

Walter took a sip of coffee. "I don't think so, but I'm not sure. Like you, I've got nothing to lose, so I might as well try."

The waiter walked up with James's breakfast as Walter hid behind his newspaper. James glanced at some headline concerning President Coolidge before he began to eat his breakfast as quickly as he could. As the waiter came back to the table to refill the water in front of the men, James asked him, "What's the closest Catholic church to the hotel?"

The waiter responded, "You don't want to go to the closest. You want to go to Gesu in downtown. It just opened and it's absolutely gorgeous." He finished refilling the glasses and walked away.

Peering over his paper, Walter chuckled and said, "Are you sure you don't want me to go? Maybe I could convince Jeanette to come to."

"I don't need a chaperone, Walter. Besides there is no guarantee she will be at that church." James stated. He looked down at his watch and realized the time, "I've got to go. See you later, Walter." James got up from the table and counted out a nice tip. He headed to the entrance of the lobby, where the cabs would be lined up. He opened the entrance door and felt the salty sea air hit his nostrils. He hoped his harebrained plan would work before walking to the nearest cab and climbing in.

"Gesu Catholic Church, please."

JAMES GAZED ACROSS the water as the cab moved across the causeway. Looking south, he wondered what Havana would be like compared to Miami. The rich history of the Rome of the Caribbean would overshadow the boom town of Miami, but James also knew that the daydream of going to Havana would never occur.

Coming back into reality as the cab entered downtown Miami, James looked out at the freshly planted palm trees and their stark contrast against the blue Miami sky. He noticed the palm trees were planted at standard intervals along the roads, giving a planned feel to the young city. Again his mind wandered to Havana and the pictures he had seen of the old city. Whereas everything about Havana seemed old from what James knew, everything in Miami was new. And evidently, that included the Gesu Catholic Church.

The cab stopped in front of a large Spanish looking edifice replete with three white arches that made James think of the Trinity. He slipped the cabbie a couple of bills before exiting the cab. James slowly walked up the steps looking around at his surroundings. Never having been to a Catholic Mass, James was nervous; however, he knew this was his best shot at finding and apologizing to Julia before the banquet tonight.

James looked at the three doors before deciding to enter through the center one. It was culture shock. Nothing looked like any church he had ever been in before. People were stopping and dipping their hands in water, but James had no idea why. Then he noticed in the front of the church there were statues everywhere, as well as a section screened off in the front. His nose was filled with the smell of incense. The art and ornamentation was much more elaborate than anything in any Presbyterian church he had been in before. James was paralyzed, not sure what to do next.

"Excuse me," a nice old lady asked as she tried to move around James. Having been jolted back to reality, James began to look for Julia. He hoped to spot her dark brown hair only to realize that every woman in the congregation had on a veil. How was he ever going to find her if he was looking from the back, he wondered. Yet he was not about to walk to the front and look for her. He at least realized enough to know that he would look ridiculous. Deciding then to look on the right side of the Nave, James walked over and began to slowly walk down the side aisle, looking on every row at the women on it. About half way down, James noticed a taller woman with dark brown hair and a white veil on her head. Almost positive the woman was Julia, James scooted into the pew and sat a body length apart from her.

Glancing at her again, James caught her exquisite eyes and smiled, realizing he was right. She rolled her eyes and shook her head before looking down and praying once again. James, never one to take a hint, scooted just a little bit closer before whispering, "I've never been to a Catholic service before. What do I need to do?"

Julia just glared at him.

James shrugged as the candlelight danced on his freckled face.

She looked at him incredulously before whispering, "Be quiet, and follow my lead."

James smiled brightly. "I can do that."

He bowed his head slightly and mimicked Julia's prayerfulness, even going so far as to get on his knees on the kneeler bench. Julia just rolled her eyes again.

Soon the music began to play and the priest, along with a deacon and a couple of altar boys, began processing down the middle aisle toward the front. The priest climbed the stairs toward the sanctuary and kissed the altar. This startled James, and he leaned toward Julia to ask, "What is the priest doing?"

Julia frowned and said in a harsh whisper, "Be quiet!"

James backed away, still curious but realizing this was not the time to ask. He began to watch whatever Julia did and mimic it. When she knelt, James knelt. When she stood, he stood. Eventually Julia thrust a book into his hands and pointed to the page. "Follow along, if you don't know Latin," she leaned in and whispered.

James did as she commanded, beginning to read the vernacular translation of the Latin while the priest was reading a passage from Isaiah. Having never heard scripture in Latin, he was fascinated and completely lost at the same time. He snuck a glance at Julia and noticed she was actually reading the Latin instead of the vernacular. Yet again, James was impressed.

After the scripture readings, the priest walked to the lectern and began to deliver a homily in English. James, surprised after hearing Latin for the first twenty minutes, leaned toward Julia and joked, "Hey - it's a language I know."

She just glared.

Julia took out a piece of paper and a pencil from her purse and wrote, "If you say one more thing, I swear I will stab you with this pencil." She slipped the paper into James's hand with a stern look. James felt the thinness of the note before opening it. He almost laughed but was smart enough to hold the chuckle in. James turned his attention to the priest, who was discussing the importance of following the example of the wise men in coming to see Jesus.

After the homily, the priest began speaking in Latin again, with Julia responding without looking in the reader while James struggled to keep up. This continued until the congregation began to stand row by row to go forward to take the Eucharist. Julia stood, and James, still mimicking Julia's actions, stood as well and began to follow her down the pew. When she noticed he was behind her, she turned around and whispered, "You can't go up there."

"What?" James asked confused.

She whispered, "You aren't allowed to partake in the Eucharist."

"Why not?" James uttered louder than he meant to.

Julia whispered sympathetically, "Sit down. I will explain later."

So James sat back down and waited as Julia walked to the front of the Nave and bowed before kneeling at the altar. After receiving the elements, Julia crossed herself with her right hand before coming to sit back down next to James and bowing her head prayerfully. James looked on still confused about what just happened but decided he did not need to do anything else to interrupt Julia. So he sat quietly and followed the rest of the service in the prayer book until the Mass ended.

As soon as the Mass ended, Julia rounded on James, "So Dr. Pashen, would you so kindly explain to me why a Presbyterian is in a Catholic Church this morning?"

Blushing, James looked down and did not say anything. This made Julia even angrier, "So you have nothing to say?"

James mumbled, "I came hoping to see you."

"I'm sorry. I didn't hear you. What did you say?"

James said it clearly this time, "I came hoping to see you and to apologize for last night."

"Apologize for last night?

"Yes. I think I may have come on a little strong for the fact that I'm married and you're practically married."

Julia thought about it for just a moment before replying, "Well couldn't you have waited until the afternoon and looked around the hotel?"

"I guess so, but this idea seemed to work."

Julia blushed slightly and began to shuffle down the pew toward the center aisle, before looking back, "Well are you coming?"

James quickly slid behind her as they headed toward the front door where the priest was greeting the morning worshipers. James whispered into Julia's ear, "So can you explain some of the aspects of the Mass?"

She turned and looked into his eyes. Warming to him, she smiled and said, "I'll be happy to answer any questions you have as long as they are not insulting."

James responded with a gleam in his eyes, "Well, what would you consider insulting?"

Julia chuckled a bit. "Well isn't finding out how insulting you are half the fun?"

James smirked and was about to respond when they came face to face with the parish priest. Wearing wire-rimmed glasses, the father extended his hand to James. "Now you two look like a wonderful couple! What brings you to Miami?"

James and Julia looked at each other and then the father before bursting into quick denials. "We aren't together," James said at the same time Julia responded, "He's already married."

The priest began apologizing, "I am so sorry! You just seem to banter like a couple."

James nodded his head in agreement as Julia rolled her eyes. "Thank you for the wonderful homily. I particularly enjoyed the Englishness of it."

Julia quickly punched James in the ribs before saying to the priest, "I apologize for my friend, father. He's a heretic."

Julia winked at the priest as he responded, "Oh! Well thank you for joining us anyway, sir," the priest snickered. "And you Miss. Blessings to you."

"Thank you, father," Julia said as she saw James's arm extended and took it as they headed towards the steps.

"So I get to ask questions now?" James asked excitedly as they began strolling down the street.

"Sure, but no insulting ones," Julia commanded.

"So why is everything in Latin?"

So proceeded the first few questions as James got a crash course introduction to the Catholic faith. Julia explained why mass was in Latin, the art in the church, and the reasons James was not allowed to partake in the Eucharist. However, everything went off the rails with question four.

"So are all Papist churches like that?"

Julia stopped and removed her hand. "Excuse me?"

James, not realizing he had done anything wrong, asked again, "So are all Papist churches like that one?"

Julia's face quickly turned red. "Do you know what you just did?"

James looked confused and answered, "No, what have I done."

"You called me a Papist. Do you not understand how insulting that is?"

James frowned as Julia continued, "By calling me that, you are basically accusing me of worshiping the pope!"

"But I hear people call Catholics that all the time."

Julia huffed and responded, "James, it's insulting! I mean, did you even hear the word pope in that service? Oh wait, of course not! Because you have been too lazy to learn Latin!"

Julia began to walk in the opposite direction of where James was standing. After a moment of shock, James ran after her. "Wait! Julia! I didn't know!" He shouted trying to catch up with her. She turned on him and glared. "You remember the rule? You insulted me, so I'm done. Have a nice day, Dr. Pashen!"

James looked at her trying to fix the situation, "At least let me get us a cab."

"There is no 'us' getting a cab. I need some time by myself. You find your own way back to the Flamingo. This 'Papist' doesn't want your help."

Chapter 7
The Banquet

JAMES CARESSED THE smooth wooden fountain pen as he thought about what to change in the speech. After a minute of silent contemplation, he began marking through and scribbling furiously on the paper that sat on the small wooden desk near the window of his room. With only a few hours until the opening banquet for the convention, he had holed himself up in the room ever since his return to the hotel after the disaster after Mass. He also knew he did not have much more time to edit the speech before it would be time to deliver it. Yet even with the deadline looming, he could not concentrate on the speech. Instead his mind kept wandering. From fretting about his future to the confrontation with Julia, his mind seemed to want to concentrate on anything but the speech before him. Frustrated with himself and his situation, he stood up from the desk and walked over to the bedside table. He thought if he read for a little bit, it would take his mind off of his own stupidity.

As he reached over to grab the book, he felt a breeze whip across his face. Glancing to the window, he noticed the flowers sitting on the bureau which reminded him of Maude.

> *Charlottesville, Virginia - February 20, 1923 -* James tapped his feet nervously as he waited for her to finish reading the manuscript. With the children in bed and his pipe in his hand, all he could do was fidget.
>
> He took a deep pull on the pipe, letting the smoke swish around his mouth. He exhaled before standing up from the rectangular dining table and going to the ice box and grabbing a Coca-Cola. He went to the bottle opener on the wall and snapped the Coca-Cola open. Sitting back down, he tried to wait patiently before finally asking, "Well?"

Maude smiled as she sipped her tea. "This is really good, James," She said without looking up from the manuscript. "There are places I would spruce up, but I've never read a perspective of the South like this."

James leaned back and let out an audible sigh that he had been holding in since he handed her the manuscript the day before.

Drawing more smoke from the pipe, James responded, "Abney will hate it."

"True, but George has always been a curmudgeon. He'll get over it."

James grabbed the Coke bottle. He sprung up from the table, and the hardwood floor of their dining room creaked as James paced back and forth. "So is the evidence convincing? Does the thesis work?" He fired off in rapid succession.

"James, calm down. It's the best work you've ever done. I honestly think you should submit it." Maude said calmly.

James stopped, stunned by what he heard.

"Submit it?"

"Yes, submit it. Remember, I read through Walter's book a few years ago when he presented at the AHA. Yours is better," Maude stated proudly.

"You're just saying that because you're my wife," James remarked skeptically.

"Remember, I grew up with a historian father and married a historian as well. I've read enough of these books to know what is good. You should submit this," she reiterated.

"Well the only issue I have left is what to name the book. Any ideas?" James asked.

"What about *Poor White Trash*?"

James sat down and contemplated all that Maude had said and what it would mean for his career if he got to present at the American Historians Association conference. He couldn't help but smile.

That same smile showed on James's face as he looked out the window with the breeze on his face. He looked down at the clock and noticing that it was 3:16, he realized he had to get back to work on the speech instead of reading. Walking back to the desk, he sat down before his smile turned to a frown. His every waking thought for thirty-nine hours was about a future he could not control and a woman who meant nothing to him. Maude had been with him through good times and bad times, through love and loss. Yet here he was running away from this uncertain future and chasing after some young woman who he had looked at a few times. James knew it had to stop. He grabbed the next page of the speech, and after making a silent vow to concentrate on the present and not the future, he began to reread the third section.

JAMES, DECKED OUT IN a black tuxedo complete with bowtie, strode into the ballroom where the banquet was being held. Although a few minutes late, his only real worry was having to sit near Julia. After vowing to himself that he needed to concentrate on the speech, he thought it would be best to avoid her.

However, his wish was short lived when he noticed Walter flagging him down. He saw who was near Walter, and he groaned audibly before walking over to the table. Walter boomed, "James, my dear boy! I saved a seat at the table for you!" James forced a smile as he looked for his seat. Seated at the table were Hugh Campbell, Jeanette Fallon, Ira Grossman, and Ira's protege, Julia. The one open chair was between Julia and Walter. James frowned slightly before sitting down and peeking over at Julia. Looking dazzling in a full length light blue gown with a low neck line, Julia glared at him when she noticed his frown. It was obvious she had seen his reaction.

James turned toward Walter and leaned in, whispering, "Did you really have to sit her next to me?"

"I thought that's what you would want," Walter responded quietly. "I thought you'd be proud of me."

James looked down to the floor as Walter raised his eyebrows. "Walter, I was only supposed to distract her for a night. Being her dinner date all week was not what I had in mind."

Walter whispered, "I just need more time with Jeanette. Besides, you went to see her this morning, I thought you might like the distraction before the big speech."

"Let's just say some things happened today to make me think your idea wasn't such a good idea after all," James whispered toward Walter.

Ira boomed from across the round table, "Let us have a share in the conversation!"

James straightened up, and looking around not sure what to say when Walter chimed in, "James and I were discussing the final draft of his speech for tomorrow."

Looking relieved at Walter's quick thinking, James added, "I figured I wouldn't bore the whole table with that."

"Nonsense!" Hugh said. "Your topic is fascinating. I never thought about the South that way before."

"Thank you," James said blushing. "But I've worked on it all afternoon. I'd really prefer to discuss anything else."

Julia chimed in bitingly, "What about Papists? We can talk about those."

James blanched but said, "I think I learned enough about that word for one day."

As James was responding, a coat-tailed waiter walked up and began to take drink orders, with the choices of tea, coffee, or punch. Starting with Walter, the waiter took each order until he came to Julia and James who both ordered the punch.

James then immediately turned to Walter and started talking about common people they both knew. James hoped that this would keep him from arguing with Julia, sensing that she was still angry about the morning. With her sitting next to him, he could sense a pull that naturally made him gravitate to her, but he knew he had to resist it. At least she is angry with me, he thought, maybe that will continue throughout the week.

As the punch was brought and a Waldorf Salad was placed in front of each person, James turned towards his plate and picked up his fork. Julia, angry now both from the incident this morning and from James ignoring her for the first part of the meal, leaned to his shoulder and shouted quietly, "So I call baloney on what you said earlier."

"WHAT?"

"Baloney! You were talking about me when you were whispering to Dr. Shafer," she whispered furiously.

James grimaced but admitted, "Okay, you're right. I was talking about you. Happy?"

"Not really. I would think after you chased me halfway around Miami this morning that you might actually like sitting beside me at dinner," Julia spat.

James turned slightly toward her to send a jibe back but was struck dumb when her hypnotizing eyes caught his. He stared for a moment as if mesmerized, but she broke the spell with another biting comment, "So really you were just bored this morning and thought you'd hit on the pretty young woman in her church, just for kicks?"

Stuttering, James spoke. "Of course not!"

"And where you told me I had the most beautiful eyes you've ever seen, I guess that was just a line?" Julia said firing up even more, to the point where the rest of the table began to stare at them.

"What the hell!?! I said something I know nothing about, but I didn't mean it offensively. What else am I supposed to do?!"

Julia grimaced and leaned away and spoke to the rest of the table, "If you all would excuse me, I need some fresh air."

Julia rose from her chair, grabbed her purse, and walked gracefully out toward the balcony with her dress flowing behind her from the breeze coming through the door. James buried his face into his hands before rubbing his head. Walter said, loud enough for the whole table to hear, "What did you do to that woman?"

James decided to leave the question alone. "If you all would excuse me, I believe Miss O'Connor and I need to clear the air."

James got to his feet and began slowly walking the same way Julia did toward the balcony. Taking out his pipe, he lit the tobacco as he arrived at the balcony door. Leaning against the doorway, he admired her figure in the fading sunlight as he took a puff on the pipe. Against his better judgement, James closed the distance between them and leaned against the edge of the balcony next to her. They gazed toward the peaceful movement of the ocean water hitting the beach.

After a few moments of neither moving, James whispered softly, "Julia."

"Oh, so you are acknowledging my existence now?" She said sarcastically, but with less bite than earlier.

"Will you allow me to explain?"

She turned toward him, and with her expressive eyes, looked into his and said, "This ought to be good."

James frowned. "I understand the sarcasm, but we can either discuss this as adults or I will walk back into the ballroom and this can be done."

Julia put her hand on his arm, and said, "I'm sorry."

"Thank you," James stated. "After our argument, I came back to the hotel to work on my speech for tomorrow. However, I kept thinking about last night and this morning and how I had upset you. But then I began to think about my wife, Maude, and I thought about my vows and how I have never broken them."

"And why are you telling me this?" Julia asked, although more calm than she had been a few moments before.

"Because I meant what I said last night. Because I hoped to find you at that church, not just to apologize but to simply to be in your presence. There is something about you, Julia, that draws me like a moth to a flame," James explained.

"But then why ignore me?"

"Because I need to avoid you. Don't you understand? If I don't avoid you I won't be able to stay away from you. So was I ignoring you? Yes, I was. But it was because if I don't ignore you, I'm not sure what will happen."

Julia thought about James's confession.

James looked deep into her mesmerizing eyes, hoping she would understand that he was being completely honest with her.

"You're my Medusa."

"So you're about to be petrified or do I look like I have snakes coming out of my head?"

"Both actually," James joked.

Exasperated, Julia rolled her eyes.

James pleaded, "I know you are engaged and I'm married, but if I am around you, all I'm going to do is fall further. I certainly didn't mean to anger you."

Julia, looking into his blue eyes, calmly replied, "I understand, but you need to understand one thing. Just don't ignore me. There is nothing more insulting and degrading than to be treated like I am not there. I receive that enough from men who don't think I can do this job. I don't need it from someone who professes to actually like who I am, or at least what he knows of me."

Julia grabbed her engraved cigarette case from her purse and took out a cigarette. Tapping it on her case, she then placed it in her black holder before James lit it for her, and they both smoked in silence for a moment. The tension eased between them as the smoke relaxed them.

James extended his hand, saying, "Friends?"

Julia took it and looked back in his eyes, "Friends."

James felt a weird charge go through him as their hands touched, but he said nothing.

They made small talk as each finished their smoke before James asked her, "Would you like to join me for dinner?"

"I'd be honored," Julia said, smiling at him.

James held out his arm for Julia, and she placed her hand into the crook of his elbow. Pulling her hand close to him, he thought that this was much better than her being angry.

AFTER A MAIN COURSE of roast beef with mashed potatoes and candied yams and the delivery of fresh orange sherbet to the table, everyone was relaxed and full. Walter, Hugh, and Ira were looking at the convention program and discussing what sessions they might go listen to tomorrow, while James, Julia, and Jeanette were discussing the early church research that Jeanette was writing into a book on the triumph of the saints.

"So wait a minute," James exclaimed. "You're telling me that this woman told her father that she couldn't be anything other than a Christian, and then was executed for it?"

"Not exactly, Dr. Pashen," Jeanette said. "But long term, that is what occurred."

"And Felicity had a child in jail, right before she was executed?"

Julia chimed in. "It's a very tragic story, and yet it also brings hope knowing that, in the face of persecution, they kept their faith."

"And that they are now the patron saints of mothers and expectant mothers," Jeanette added.

"So can you explain the whole patron saint thing again?" James asked, engaged in the conversation.

Julia patted him on the knee before she tried to explain the concept to him. Listening as he began to delight in the fresh citrus sherbet, James was beginning to understand when all was interrupted by the president of the American Historical Association.

Dr. Arnold Bland was a longtime professor at the University of Pennsylvania. Hunched over, he stood behind the podium and microphone, stating, "Welcome to the 40th annual meeting of the American Historical Association. We are thankful that our colleagues of the Southern Historical Association have joined us to have a combined meeting here in Miami, Florida."

A long round of applause rang throughout the room before Bland continued, "Before we begin, I would be remiss if I did not thank the following people.." He thanked the hotel, the cooks, the businesses, and pretty much everyone else who had ever entered the city.

James leaned over to Walter and joked, "Evidently Bland is the right word."

Walter jabbed back, "He forgot to thank Samuel for warning him about Miami."

James and Walter both started laughing until Julia shushed them both.

Walter's eyebrows went up as his face went into a smirk, but James looked sheepishly at the ground before glancing up at Julia. She had a smile on her face.

A few minutes later, Bland got to the point of the speech to introduce the keynote speakers for the four-day conference, asking them to stand when they were called. "First, we have Dr. James Pashen, Professor of Southern History from the University of Virginia. His speech topic is on the yeoman farmers of the Antebellum South. Dr. Pashen, would you please stand?"

James stood for a moment as the people clapped. When he sat back down, he noticed a surprised look on her face.

"Is your research really in the area of the poor?" She asked shocked.

"Yes, I've been fascinated by that my whole life."

Julia smiled and placed her hand on his thigh. "You know, Dr. Pashen, you have your moments. Not many of them, but you do have them."

Chapter 8
The Nightcap

AS THE DINNER WAS BREAKING up, Walter grabbed James by the arm. "My room is 605. Come by for a nightcap."

James looked at Walter confused.

"I got some good hooch. Just come on up," Walter added. "Now if you will excuse me, I think I will say goodnight to Jeanette."

James stood up at the same time Julia did. She smiled encouragingly as she said, "I really enjoyed dinner tonight, James."

"I did too! I really am fascinated with early church history now. Maybe I'll even learn Latin." He smirked.

She laughed, "I was rather rude at the church this morning."

"Yeah, but I put you in that position. I really should have waited to apologize for the night before."

"But really, there was no reason to apologize. I had a good time with you."

"So did I."

Neither said a word as the tension hung in the air before Julia stated, "Well, it's been a long two days, so I think I will head upstairs."

"Good night, Julia," James said while looking into her hazel eyes.

She blushed as she said, "Good night, James."

Julia walked away with her dress swishing behind her. James watched her leave before deciding to walk out on the balcony to have a smoke before heading upstairs to Walter's room. Stepping out into the cool night air, James breathed deeply the salty air that clung to him. Taking out his pipe, he joined the several other people enjoying their smokes and the night view of the ocean. Contemplating the first two days of the conference, he knew he needed to limit his interactions with Julia but did not want to deny this short pleasure of her company before heading back to the reality of Charlottesville and the unknown future. Frowning to himself, he decided to head up to Walter's room to enjoy a drink before bed. James slowly ambled up the stairs to the sixth floor, before turning left and walking down to room 605.

James knocked, not sure if Walter was upstairs yet when the door opened and the bushy eyebrows of Walter rose in expectancy. Moving aside so James could come in, Walter, who had already changed into striped pajamas, grabbed two glasses and poured out some Cuban rum. Walter handed James a glass and took a chair across from James.

"So what was that argument between you and Julia about?"

James leaned back and swished his rum around the glass before beginning the story. He explained his experience in the Catholic Mass as well as his questions to Julia, eventually ending with the explanation of calling Julia a Papist.

Upon hearing that, Walter spit out his rum. "You called her what?"

"A Papist."

"James, you didn't."

James took a sip of the rum and bowed his head shamefully.

"I know you've never lived in the North, so you don't know very many Catholics, but dear God son, you don't call them Papists. It's downright insulting," Walter chastised as he rubbed his forehead and furry eyebrows.

"Yes, I believe I picked up on that."

Walter shook his head before continuing, "I would guess, knowing how women operate better than you, that she was rather mad about you trying to ignore her at the table?"

"Let's say that didn't help the situation any, but I think we've come to an understanding."

Walter refilled his glass and offered more to James, who declined knowing he had to make his big speech in the morning.

"So what about Maude?"

James shifted in his seat and answered, "Why do you ask about Maude?"

"You know she is like a sister to me, and I know I encouraged you the other night at the speakeasy, but you sure are paying an awful lot of attention to this girl."

James exhaled and decided to tell the truth, "Well, before dinner I had vowed to myself that I was going to concentrate on the speech and not worry about Julia. You saw how long that lasted. For some reason the woman acts like a magnet pulling me toward her."

Walter looked contemplatively at James before responding, "I've had that happen a couple of times in my life. I understand. I really do. I just don't want you to hurt yourself or Maude."

"Honestly, neither do I, Walter. But tonight at dinner I realized that if I'm in her presence I will naturally be drawn to her. Hopefully I won't be Icarus to her sun."

"That's all we can hope for, and for this week to go by as quickly as possible," Walter added. "Just make me a promise."

James looked at Walter warily. "What?"

"If anything happens, it ends before you leave Miami. I won't tell Maude as long as whatever happens here ends here."

"Now you are sounding like Samuel," James joked.

"Just promise me, ok. No hurting Maude in this."

"Walter, I promise."

Walter let out an audible sigh and responded, "Ok."

Walter pulled out two cigars and offered one to James. As a cool breeze eased its way through the window, the men began to discuss Walter's infatuation with Dr. Fallon and his possibilities with her. Walter bounced ideas off of James to see his reaction before settling on a course of action to get Jeanette to notice him. James could not remember the last time Walter was that excited about a woman. James smiled to himself as he finished his cigar, and after thanking Walter for both the drink and the Cuban, he headed to his room to get ready for bed.

JAMES LAID ON HIS BACK staring at the ceiling. A bundle of nerves clinching his stomach, he could not seem to fall to sleep. The speech, Julia, and Maude all kept swirling in his brain. Turning on his side and staring at the clock that said 11:02, James knew that falling asleep was still a ways away, which made him panic even more because the most important speech of his life was in twelve hours.

Swinging around and putting his feet on the floor, James stood and filled some water into a glass. He walked over to the open window with the textured glass in hand. Sipping it slowly, he tried to think what would settle his mind.

What usually helped him relax was talking through things with Maude but he couldn't do that. She had always been the voice of sense when he was nervous or panicked. But tonight he was on his own.

Pipe in hand, James looked out on the horizon at the moon. With a new moon and barely any light coming from it, James instead turned to God. He began to pray silently, asking for clarity and peace of mind as he prepared for tomorrow. By the time his prayer was finished, he felt inspired to write Maude.

So James walked over to the desk and took out the stationary and decided to write a letter.

January 6, 1924

Dear Maude,

So I know I just wrote you last night, but I was thinking about you tonight, and I couldn't sleep. So I hoped that by writing you, I would be able to calm down and be ready for the speech tomorrow. I blame you for my nervousness, darling. If you had never convinced me to submit that damned proposal, I would never have been here in this hotel room fretting about it without you. Yet here I am.

In all seriousness, thank you for believing in me. Your expectations of me push me to new heights, and I'm so thankful for that. Tomorrow's speech could completely change our lives, and I hope you are ready for that.

Tonight was the banquet to open the convention. The food was ok, although the orange sherbet was perhaps the best I've ever had. The President of the AHA, a Dr. Bland, droned on and on but he did recognize me as one of the keynote speakers, which was kind of nice. Walter and I ate with a couple of people from the University of Chicago. You'd love Dr. Grossman. He has asked to meet you, so I told him he was welcome to come to Charlottesville anytime he liked. We probably wouldn't want to have him when your mother is around, as he is a bit more fancy than your mother would accept. But he's a great guy. He brought his star student to the convention this year, whose specialty is early Christian history. We have had several conversations and the research is fascinating.

Anyhow, I hope your family is well in Knoxville, and that the kids are behaving. I'm looking forward to seeing you all next week.

Affectionately yours,

James

James scanned over the note one more time before folding it neatly and placing it in an envelope that he addressed to his wife. James wished he had accepted that second drink from Walter, thinking that maybe the rum could help him relax. Instead, he decided he would shower before laying down for the night.

Day 3
Monday, January 7, 1924

Chapter 9
The Speech

JAMES CUT A PIECE OF his fried eggs with a fork while reading over the speech one more time. Having put on his best gray suit and red tie, he was careful as he brought the fork to his mouth. Even though his hard fried eggs were done just right, he was so nervous he was barely able to keep his breakfast down. Walter sat across from James enjoying the spectacle. Walter exuded relaxation as he crossed his legs and read the newspaper. After taking in the show for a couple of minutes, Walter decided to put James out of his misery.

"James," Walter muttered.

When James didn't answer, Walter spoke louder, "James!"
"What?" James stated frustratingly.
"Look at me."

"Walter, I don't have time for this. I have to give the speech in an hour, and I'm still not ready."
"James, the speech is done. There is nothing more you can do to it."
"But..."
Walter interrupted. "Listen to me."
James stopped talking and put his elbows on the table.
"You researched for two years. You took a year to the write the book. You are the leading expert in the field of the average southerner. There is nothing more you can do to be ready for the speech in an hour, so have a little coffee." Walter said as he pushed a cup of coffee over to James.

James frowned. "Let me do this one more thing, plus I don't enjoy coffee."

Disappointed that James would not listen to him, Walter decided to take a drastic measure. He began to scan the dining room when he noticed Jeanette and Julia eating breakfast on the other side of a column. Walter knew that Julia would distract James for the next hour, so he caught Dr. Fallon's eyes and after smiling at her, motioned them to come join James and him at the table. As the ladies walked to the table, dressed for business in knee high skirts and jackets that fell to the length of the skirt, Walter smiled and grabbed Julia by the hand. He whispered something into her ear which made her smile. She sat down next to James and immediately grabbed the speech and handed it to Walter.

"What are you doing?!?" James exclaimed.

Julia smiled and looked at him. "Walter said you needed to relax, so I took the speech so you can't work on it anymore."

"But, I need…"

Julia put her hand on James's knee which made him quiet down. "James, it's finished, and I'm sure it will be wonderful."

"But just…"

Julia smiled, "Let it go."

James leaned back and took a deep breath. "Ok, well can I at least have a Coca-Cola then?"

Walter flagged down a waiter to get James a soda as he asked, "Would you like anything added to it?"

James looked confused for a second until Walter flashed his flask toward him.

Jeanette jumped in and noted, "I always have a glass before speaking. It calms the nerves."

Walter raised his eyebrows in appreciation as James stated, "Sure then. I need to calm down."

As the waiter walked over, Julia asked James what he had done after the banquet. Constantly shifting in his chair, he proceeded to talk about drinking with Walter then working on the speech before bed.

After Walter placed the order for the soda, the table began to discuss the day's news. Walter grabbed the soda when the waiter arrived. Once the waiter was gone, Walter put a little rum into the drink and stirred it before handing it to James, who was now tapping his right foot. "Now drink this and then tell us a story about your childhood."

"What?" James said, dumbfounded.

"Just trust me."

So James grabbed the Coca-Cola and took a long sip. The rum burned his throat but immediately released his tension. Noticing that all three people were staring at him, he decided to follow Walter's command.

"I guess this story was sometime in 1894 because I remember being eight years old. So my brother Howard and I decided that we wanted to learn how to use dad's rifle. Since I was the oldest, I convinced Howard to sneak into the bedroom and get the rifle out of the closet. Now our house was located just outside of Eufaula, Alabama where my dad owned the local general store. We had some land since we lived just outside of town, so we decided we'd use the back steps to place the gun down since neither of us were able to hold up the rifle. So anyway, here I was, under the steps with the hunting rifle, trying to figure out what you do next when my little sister, Clara begins to walk down the stairs. Now because she is only three, we didn't see or hear her as we are under the stairs. We finally figure out how to use the gun and it fires, right as Clara steps on the same step the rifle is sitting on. She falls down the stairs, as my mother comes running out of the house screaming, 'Clara's been shot! Clara's been shot! Oh God! Oh God!' Howard and I take off for the woods, hoping our mother doesn't get a hold of us. We hide in the woods and watch, knowing that we couldn't have shot Clara since the end of the rifle was past the stairs. So we waited about three or four hours before we walk back to the house, hoping my mother calmed down. Let's just say that afternoon, my mother whipped me worse than I ever had gotten whipped before or since."

James took another nip from the rum and cola while the other three at the table laughed heartily. For the next bit, the others each shared a childhood story before Walter handed him the speech. "Go knock 'em dead."

James stood and was about to walk away when Julia stood as well and came up beside him. She touched his arm and drew him into her eyes before softly saying, "Good luck."

His entire spirit lifted as he walked toward the ballroom.

"WELCOME TO DAY ONE of the 40th annual meeting of the American Historians Association," Arnold Bland called out to the full ballroom. "We are happy you are here today for our opening keynote address. Today, our topic is "Common Folk in the Old South," and to introduce our keynote speaker, I am pleased to present the Head Professor of History at the Alabama Polytechnic Institute, Dr. George Pickett Abney."

Dr. Abney, his ever-present cane clacking with every other step, walked up to the podium, and after propping his cane against the stand, he began, "Thank you for the opportunity to introduce our keynote speaker for the morning. Dr. James Pashen is the Professor of Southern History at the University of Virginia. A former student of mine at Alabama Polytechnic Institute, he received his master's degree at Vanderbilt University before gaining his doctorate at the College of William and Mary. With his research focus on the average southerner prior to the War Between the States, James offers a fresh viewpoint on both what it means to be a southerner, but also what it means to be an American. I am honored, as his mentor, to introduce to you Dr. James Pashen."

As his fellow historians began to applaud, James walked across the dias toward Dr. Abney. Smiling, Dr. Abney hugged him and whispered, "I'm proud of you son." James teared up as he heard George's cane tapping away as Dr. Abney sat back down.

James placed his speech down onto the podium and looked around the room. Packed full of historians from across the country, James realized he had reached the pinnacle of his profession, the goals he had aspired for since his first class with Dr. Abney back in 1905. He had made it.

Which instead of speaking, made him step back and take a breath. What was next? What else could he accomplish? The thoughts froze him, and he looked around again. He saw the most important historians in the United States staring at him. How could he, a small town boy from Eufaula, Alabama, be on this stage? He spotted Walter frowning at him and Ira Grossman looking worried. He continued his silence as his eyes scanned the room until they fell on Julia. She looked at him, and instead of looking worried, she smiled the most brilliant smile he had ever seen and mouthed, "I have faith in you."

Taking one more deep breath, James stepped to the podium and began, "In 1847, in the town of Jackson, Alabama..."

"AND ALTHOUGH THE LAST seventy years of historiography seemed to focus on the history of planters and their ties to slavery, I hope you have seen the importance of the common man in relation to both the antebellum South and these United States. Thank you for your time."

James stepped away from the podium as the room broke into loud applause. He smiled and turned around and began shaking hands with the people on the dias, stopping at Dr. Abney who, bursting with pride, gave out a rebel yell. James laughed, relieved that the speech had gone over well as he gave his first mentor a big hug.

"I would have never been here without you," James said.

Dr. Abney pulled back and looked at him misty-eyed, "Maude would be so proud!"

"Thank you, sir."

As the room began to disburse to smaller meetings, James began to take the steps down from the stage to go have a smoke when a grey-haired man in a rich white suit came up and introduced himself. "Dr. Pashen, I'm William Taylor and I loved the speech. Your point about the importance of free blacks in the antebellum South is an idea that I had never thought about before."

"Thank you, sir," James replied as he shook Taylor's hand.

"I have a home here in Miami and am having some people over this evening for a small party. I would love for you and your wife to join us for the evening. Several friends of mine are down for the winter and it should be a fun night of drinks and food."

"I'd love to come, but my wife did not travel with me to Miami."

Taylor shrugged, "Then bring someone else! I'm sure you can find a woman to be your date for the night."

James contemplated the possibility for a moment before responding, "Thank you for the invitation. Can you give me the address?"

Taylor handed James a card with the address on it, and after telling James he hoped to see him tonight, Taylor walked out of the ballroom.

James stood stunned that one of the chief executives of Harvest National would invite him to his house. Yet now, James had to find a date.

Walking out of the ballroom toward the lobby, James had no idea where Walter went, but he knew he needed advice on whether he should ask someone or decide not to go. He knew there was only one person he could ask, but knew that wasn't the best idea. Quickly scanning the lobby, he noticed Walter smoking a cigar and talking with Ira, Jeanette and Julia. He walked quickly over and joined them.

Although James had walked over to talk to Walter, he realized when he got to them that he only had eyes for Julia. She smiled and told him, "That was a wonderful speech, James!"

"Thank you!" James responded blushingly.

James tore his eyes away from Julia and asked Walter, "Do you have any plans for the evening?"

"Actually, I do, my good man," Walter said grinning ear to ear at Jeanette. "Dr. Fallon here has been so kind as to accept my invitation to dinner."

James looked impressed before stating, "Well, what about you, Ira? Any plans for tonight?"

"I do! There is an informal dinner between some other professors of my type and we always have a good time every year," Ira answered.

James turned his attention to Julia, and against his better judgement said, "And do you have any plans for the evening?"

She looked appraisingly and said, "Why do you ask?"

"Well, I've been invited to a dinner this evening and it requires a date. What are you doing at six?"

Chapter 10
The Mansion

AT FIVE AFTER SIX, James stood tapping his feet impatiently waiting for Julia to come downstairs. Food would not be served until nine, so he knew they had plenty of time, but he was nervously eager to spend the evening with her. Dressed in a black vested suit with a red Macclesfield tie, he stood by the fireplace smoking his pipe. Leaning on the mantle, James enjoyed the smell of burning wood as he gazed into the dancing flames of the fireplace in the lobby contemplating the night ahead. He had heard that Taylor's home, Vizcaya, was the most beautiful in all of Florida, and that the property had a pool, gardens, a dock, as well as many other things to distract or entertain.

While still staring at the fire, Julia walked up wearing a gold dress with lace shoulders straps. A golden sparkling headband adorned her dark brown hair and a two-tiered necklace hung down the front of her dress. Holding a brown coat in her left hand, she touched James's arm to get his attention. As he looked up his jaw dropped before he blurted out, "You look stunning!"

Julia blushed slightly and smiled, "Thank you!"

She took a cigarette out of her gold case and tapped it twice. She brought the black holder to her mouth before James flicked his engraved lighter and lifted it to Julia's cigarette. After taking a deep drag, Julia asked, "So what is this place we are going to this evening?"

"It's called Vizcaya, it is the vacation home of William Taylor."

"The industrialist?"

"Yes, that's him."

Julia thought for a moment, "I think he's given quite a bit of money to the University of Chicago."

"Well he loved the speech and that's how I got the invitation. So are you ready to go?" James asked.

She smiled and handed him her coat, which he helped her put on. James extended his arm to escort her to a cab. Julia placed her left hand on his elbow as they exited the lobby.

"So how were the other forums you went to today?" James asked Julia as the bellhop flagged down a cab. Julia began to discuss the Women's History forum she attended as the cab pulled up and the bellhop opened the door for them.

As they climbed into the cab, James noticed that their driver was again Samuel, who recognized James immediately by joking with him, "Mr. James, it's you again!"

James smiled in response, "It seems we keep meeting."

Julia appeared confused at the exchange before James began the introduction, "Julia, this is my personal driver, Samuel. Samuel, this is Julia, my date for the evening."

"Oh date for the evening, huh?" Samuel looked reproachfully at James.

James shrugged while Julia observed the exchange with a sense of uncertainty. James leaned over and whispered, "I'll tell you later."

"So Samuel, could you take us to Vizcaya. The address is…"

"Vizcaya, I don't need the address," Samuel said confidently as they pulled away from the hotel and headed toward the causeway.

Julia leaned over to James and whispered, "So how often have you been in this cab?"

"Well, this is either the third or fourth time Samuel's driven me in the past few days."

"That explains the familiarity but not the frown."

James chuckled and whispered, "Well, he gave Walter and me a warning on the first night that Miami can lead people into losing who they are and not to let the place change them. So I assume the frown is because he is unhappy that I ignored him."

Julia wondered, "What do you mean, you ignored him?"

"Well, I am on a date with you, aren't I?" James said cheekily.

"Indeed you are. So taking young single women out on dates isn't normal for you?"

James chuckled, "Let's just say this is a first for me, and Samuel may not be that happy about it."

As James smirked at her, Samuel looked back and asked, "So what takes you out to Vizcaya?"

"Mr. Taylor invited us to a party at the house this evening," James replied.

"Oh a Vizcaya party! Those are the best in Miami!" Samuel gushed. "Usually there will be famous people, music, and maybe even a film after dinner! The parties are legendary. You'll love it there. But temptation will also surround you. Heed my words."

James and Julia smiled at each other before James responded, "You make it sound like Sodom and Gomorrah."

Samuel replied ominously, "It can be. Don't forget my advice, Mr. James."

AS THE CAB SPED DOWN the drive toward the mansion, James and Julia gasped at the view. In front of the cab was this beautiful Mediterranean Revival mansion, with a striking red roof covering the three story white home. They looked around and noticed the backdrop of palm trees and the Atlantic Ocean. The house was perfectly situated to create a sense of wonder. They noticed a set of stairs led up to the front of the house as the car drove around a perfectly manicured circular driveway. They were in awe, neither having ever seen anything quite like it.

"I've seen plantation homes and city mansions but nothing quite like this," James muttered in awe.

Samuel pulled the car around to a couple of servants who opened the car door and paid the cab fare before James could pull out his money clip. He looked at Julia and shrugged before exiting the cab. Right before getting out, he asked Samuel, "Can you pick us up at one?"

"Of course, Mr. James, I will see you then."

James smiled as he got out of the car and felt Julia grab his elbow. The salt-filled air hit their nostrils as he turned towards her, he looked into her eyes and said, "I hope you'll have a great night tonight."

"I'm sure I will."

They began to ascend the steps toward the open front doors when Mr. Taylor, still in his white suit, came down to meet them. "Dr. Pashen! I'm so glad you could make it. And who is this beautiful woman?" Taylor said as he took Julia's hand.

"Mr. Taylor, this is Julia O'Connor. She is from your hometown of Chicago," James stated as Mr. Taylor kissed Julia's hand.

"Miss O'Connor, you are welcome here at Vizcaya. Anything you need this evening, please let me know," Taylor noted, charming her and making her smile. "Dr. Pashen and Miss O'Connor, drinks are being served in the courtyard. You are welcome to walk around the house and the gardens. Music is on the back patio. Dinner will be served at nine. Again, please let me know if you need anything, and enjoy Vizcaya!"

Taylor then continued down the steps as the couple walked into the lobby of the mansion. Two more servants, dressed in coattails, took both James's and Julia's jackets before pointing out where they could get drinks. They examined the statue of Bacchus and walked into the courtyard to the bar. After being handed two drinks, they decided to walk through the house, heading to the living room first.

"So what are we actually doing here?" Julia questioned as they walked onto the gray marble floor of the living room. "I don't know about you, but I feel completely out of my element."

James was silent for a moment as he looked around the packed room; there were people sitting on every bit of furniture, and many of them enjoying drinks as James took a sip of his bourbon. A dark red and black rug hung on the wall and accented the speckled dark gray floor. James relished the warming amber in his mouth and swallowed it slowly before answering, "I am here because Mr. Taylor invited me, and he is the kind of man who I wouldn't dare refuse anything. You are here because there is no one in Miami I'd rather experience this with."

"Fair enough," Julia stated, taking a sip of her highball. "But I did notice I was the third person you asked what they were doing tonight."

James chuckled but answered, "Because I knew I shouldn't ask you, but that doesn't mean I didn't want to."

She smiled and led James to the marble-carved fireplace where she turned and asked, "Do you know what these symbols on the fireplace mean?"

Looking over the mantle, he knew he was lost, so he turned and admitted he knew nothing. Julia touched his arm lightly and began to explain each of the symbols carved into the mantle. As she turned her head, she saw the massive pipe organ with a painting of the Holy Family above the organ.

"Oh, it's Mary!" Julia said darting off to examine the painting. James walked behind her taking another sip. With a glowing smile, Julia turned to James.

"I love Mary! She's my queen!"

"So can I ask a question that I promise I don't mean in an offensive way?" James asked hesitantly, remembering the Papist argument of the day before.

Julia tilted her head and eyed him suspiciously, "I will reserve judgement on whether your question is offensive or not."

"Well, I want to understand the Catholic connection to Mary. I know you all don't actually worship Mary or anything, but I don't know..." James trailed off hoping he had not displeased her.

"And why, pray tell, did you think that would be offensive?"

"Because I don't know how to word things."

Julia smirked before replying, "You do have a point there."

James shrugged his shoulders before Julia, looking up at the painting, began to answer, "Mary is just grand! She is the only one in the Bible who will put Jesus in his place. You know the story of Jesus's first miracle in John? You know why he did it? Because his mother told him to. Catholics see Mary as the one person who can talk to Jesus about anything, so we ask Mary to intervene with Jesus for us. People think we pray to Mary, but what we are doing is praying that Mary will intercede with Jesus for us."

James contemplated this viewpoint while they continued to stare at the painting of the Holy Family when Julia noticed, "I bet this was an altarpiece at one time, and if so, I can't believe they cut it in half for decoration!"

Overhearing their conversation a man nearby butted into the conversation, "And what exactly is the problem with the altarpiece, Miss?"

Julia, with fire in her eyes, responded, "The painting was obviously created for a church setting, probably Catholic, and Mr. Taylor had it cut in half!"

The man jabbed back, "And does this room look better with that painting there or would you rather see the pipes from the organ, because believe me, I could have left the room that way!"

"Why couldn't you leave the altarpiece as it was originally made?" Julia asked argumentatively.

"Because Miss..."

"O'Connor." Julia said huffily.

"Because Miss O'Connor, we still have to access the pipes to repair them. And, as you will see later when we watch the movie, the pipes are an important part of the experience here at Vizcaya," the man stated calmly. "By the way, I am Louis Ververs, chief architect and art director for the house."

Ververs extended his hand to Julia, took hers and kissed it. Julia grinned as Ververs continued, "You've got moxie, Miss O'Connor. I'd love to introduce you to my partner."

"By all means, lead the way," Julia responded grabbing James's elbow.

They walked across the room next to the Admiral carpet that hung down the wall. Standing there was a beefy man with a huge cigar talking with an older couple.

Ververs broke into the conversation and pulled his partner aside.

"Miss O'Connor, this is my partner, Julius Coy."

Once the pleasantries were exchanged, Ververs continued, "We live on a boat on the harbor. You've got a lot of spunk, Miss O'Connor. You're welcome to come join us for drinks anytime."

Julia, blushing from the praise, smiled, "Thank you for the invite, but I will be here only a couple more days before heading back to Chicago."

"Well I'm sorry to hear that," Ververs noted. "By the way, Mr. Pashen, this is one fine girl you've got here."

"I agree, Mr. Ververs."

Ververs smiled before saying, "Well, I'm going to get some more drinks, if you have any questions, please feel free to find me and ask."

Julia beamed as she called after him, "We will!"

AN HOUR LATER, AFTER walking around the mansion, and examining the rooms that were open, James and Julia found themselves on the East Terrace sipping on their third drinks and overlooking the bay. As the warm winter breeze blew off the bay, they found themselves in a conversation with Mr. Taylor and Lillian Gish, a famous actress whose newest movie the guests would be watching later that evening.

As Taylor grilled James on the study of free blacks in the antebellum South, the actress and Julia were discussing the Gish's most famous film, *The Birth of a Nation*, and the social implications of the Civil War and Reconstruction. During the conversations, a person with a camera came up to Mr. Taylor and whispered in his ear. Mr. Taylor piped up, "Let's get together for a picture. My photographer likes to keep a record of our guests."

So James and Julia stood next to each other as James wrapped his arm around her. She looked up at him and smiled before staring at the camera. A moment later and the photograph of the four of them was taken. After thanking Mr. Taylor, the photographer moved to a different section of the terrace. Shortly after, the band on the portico began to play some music. Several couples began to wander toward the middle of the terrace and began to dance.

James looked at Mr. Taylor and said, "Excuse me, sir, but I would like to dance with my date for a bit."

"By all means, young man. Enjoy yourself!"

So James proffered his hand to Julia who smiled as she accepted it. They walked to where the others were dancing. James pulled her near, and they began to slowly twirl around the terrace.

"It's so beautiful out here," Julia said, glancing around as the new moon slowly crept into the night sky..

James pulled her closer and held her hand tight. After a couple of minutes, Julia stated, "You could have danced with the most famous woman in America. She was standing right with us, and yet you asked me to dance. I just don't understand why."

He did not immediately answer, but instead continued to move with the music. Then he pulled his head away from her cheek to look her in the eyes, "I asked the person I wanted to dance with. She may be famous and she may be beautiful, but she's not you."

Julia attempted to laugh off the compliment, "Now James, you barely know me, and yet here you are turning down the chance to dance with the most beautiful woman in the world."

"Who said I turned down the chance to dance with the most beautiful woman in the world?" James asked seriously.

Patting his upper chest with her left hand, she said playfully, "Be serious."

Still moving slowly to the music of the string quartet, James asked solemnly, "Julia, do you try to dissuade every man who pays attention to you?"

"Since I am engaged, yes I usually do."

"Well, I don't scare easily," James said.

He pulled her near his cheek as the quartet began to play another song. After a few minutes of silence, James shifted to look into her eyes. He became intoxicated by her closeness before moving a hand to her cheek and caressing her face.

However, before he could do anymore, Julia's hand came up quickly and slapped him. She angrily walked off the terrace and into the garden on the south side of the mansion.

Chapter 11
The Garden

JAMES'S FACE STUNG while he watched Julia stalk away into the vast garden. Looking around hoping no one saw, he noticed Mr. Taylor chuckling at him. With his head down, James walked over to him.

"Son," he said putting his arm around James. "Why are you standing here with me?"

James appeared defeated as he asked, "Where else should I be?"

"Chasing after her, of course! It's obvious you carry a torch for her, so what are you waiting for?"

"Mr. Taylor, I'm married and she's engaged," James said, matter of factly.

"Look over there," Taylor stated, pointing toward the other side of the terrace. "See that woman over there?"

James observed a fifty-something year old woman with short black hair, holding a wine glass, and wearing a dark tan mid-length dress.

Taylor continued, "See her husband next to her? They stay in the guest room that is secretly connected to my room because she is my long-term lover. He knows nothing about it, and we plan to keep it that way. My point though is that we love each other, and we never would have gotten to that point if I hadn't pursued her when I fell."

James looked back at the woman and her husband and asked Taylor, "What about her husband? What about him?"

"He gets to enjoy Vizcaya a few weeks each year, and has a doting wife for 11 months a year," Taylor explained matter-of-factly. "I may only get a few weeks a year with her, but I get a few weeks with the woman I love. Go to Miss O'Connor. Talk to her. You never know."

James began to argue, "But..."

"No buts. Just go to her. Woo her. Find out if there's a chance she could love you. You will never regret it. I promise."

James thought for a moment before smiling and thanking Mr. Taylor. He then walked purposefully around the terrace and down into the garden looking for Julia. As his eyes began to scan around, James was amazed to see the layout of the garden. It looked like something out of a photo book of an old European palace. Bushes, trees, and benches everywhere, all perfectly manicured and placed. A sea of green surrounded him, and he had no idea where to begin to find Julia.

He walked down the steps to the garden and began to slowly look at the bushes and flowers that populated the area. Having no real history with horticulture, James had no idea what species the plants were. He walked passed revelers carrying drinks and a few couples using the secluded areas to become more familiar. Eventually, James decided to go into the Theater Garden. He overheard a couple arguing furiously about the woman feeling ignored during the evening. Rolling his eyes, realizing that soon could be him, James snuck away, deciding to look next in the Maze Garden.

James entered the maze area and saw her sitting on the back garden bench. She looked up and he smiled at her, but she only put her head back down. He walked around the bushes set in a labyrinth and sat down next to her, but held his tongue. He just enjoyed the view while sitting next to her.

Eventually Julia looked up and asked, "Why did you try to kiss me?"

James shook his head and rolled his eyes. He answered, "Isn't the answer obvious?"

"But you're married. I'm engaged. This can't be anything!" Julia tried to convince herself.

"But what if it is something?"

The question hung in the air as Julia breathed slowly. The music from the terrace drifted over the garden as they sat side-by-side in contemplation.

After a minute, Julia turned and asked earnestly, "And what do you think this is or can be?"

"I don't know, Julia. But I want to find out." James replied.

He reached out and grabbed her left hand. "What I know is this. It's been a long time since I was goofy for someone like I am you. I'll admit that I started paying attention to you to help Walter have time with Dr. Fallon, but the more I talk to you and the more time I spend with you, the goofier I get. I know that we only have a few days together before we go our separate ways, but I want to use these few days to spend as much time with you as I possibly can."

Julia sat quietly thinking about what James had said. He stared forward at the garden. A light breeze blew the salt air through the trees while they sat in silence.

"James," Julia said, breaking the silence. "I have to level with you. I am not sure about anything right now. I agree that something is here between us. But I'm insured and I love my fiance. He is everything to me, and I can't think of my life without him."

"I am not asking you to give up your fiance. I certainly don't plan on declaring independence from my wife. But I will regret forever if I don't find out what is between us. I'm not asking you to make whoopie or anything like that. But for the next three days, I want to spend every moment I can with you."

Still caressing her hand, James looked at her hopefully. She turned and said, "I need to think about this."

"I understand. Do you just want to enjoy tonight? I promise not to try to kiss you again."

Julia squeezed his hand as she said, "That sounds like a wonderful idea."

THEY WALKED HAND-IN-hand farther away from the house and toward the mound on the opposite end of the garden. As they climbed to the top, a white marbled building stood overlooking a stunning blue lagoon. James and Julia were both silent as they stood overlooking the lagoon, enjoying the physical presence of the other.

They stood at the railing, holding hands when James asked her, "So what was the last book you read?"

Julia beamed and turned toward him. "Well because of fall classes, I didn't get much time to read anything I wanted to. Over Christmas though, I read several books, but the last one I read was *One of Ours* by Willa Cather."

"I read that last year as well. What was your opinion on it?"

"Well, I could really connect with the first part. This man who seemed to have everything laid out for him, and to feel stifled by that reality. However, I felt that the book goes off the rails a bit when you get to the war section. I'm sure there are people who find who they are at war, but the book almost glorifies war in a way that I find appalling."

James mulled over her point of view before responding, "See, I think all people feel like Claude sometimes. They get stuck in life and can't find a way to change their situation. The drudgery of everyday life weighs them down and there seems to be no escape."

"But is war really the method to find your way out?"

"Do we get to choose our ways out, or do the ways choose us?" James pondered aloud. "And maybe war is not the best, but sometimes people are so desperate to get out of the mundaneness of their everyday life, that they choose things that aren't the best for them in order to get them out of their quiet desperation."

Julia pondered this thought as they walked down the steps toward the fountain portion of the garden. "So this is a personal question, but am I your Great War?"

"Pardon?" James replied, knowing full well what she was asking, but not sure how to respond. Instead he led them to the edge of the fountain and looked at the marble edifice.

"Am I your Great War? Am I your way to get out of the mundaneness of everyday life? Because if that is the case, we can end this date right now, because I promise you that I am not the answer to your 'quiet desperation.'"

James grabbed her other hand and turned her to face him. Staring into her eyes, James replied, "Julia, I had NO plans to fall for anyone, or do anything to get out of my everyday life. I came to Miami to give a speech and drink with Walter. You just happened to be at the speakeasy Saturday night."

"But what if it had been some other young woman at the speakeasy? Maybe some pretty little protestant thing, with a short bob and nice gams. I'm sure there are plenty of them around these parts," Julia huffed jealously.

Exasperated, James dropped her hands and walked a few feet away before turning back around and saying, "I wasn't looking for someone, Julia. You just showed up and I fell because you are you. I promise you, I wouldn't be on a date with anyone else."

James reached for her hand again, and she placed hers in his. They quietly walked around the fountain, listening to the water splash. Julia asked, "So tell me, since you asked Catholic questions, can I ask a Calvinist one?"

"Sure! What do you want to know?"

"Can you explain predestination to me?" Julia asked.

"No." James blurted out.

Julia frowned then James responded again. "I'll try my best but it was never my favorite theological doctrine."

Hand in hand, they walked slowly back toward the mansion with James butchering the doctrine of predestination.

Dinner would be served soon.

"THAT WAS INCREDIBLE!" Julia exclaimed to Mr. Taylor after the most incredible meal of her life. "I've never tasted such mouthwatering delights."

"Thank you Miss O'Connor! I am quite proud of my staff and their abilities to please. I hope you two are planning to stay for the movie. I even brought in an organist from New York to be able to play for us," Mr. Taylor said.

"Yes, we are planning on it," James said as he took another sip of bourbon.

"Well the movie will start in about ten minutes in the courtyard, as soon as the servants have the chairs set up," Taylor added. "And make sure you refresh your drinks."

Taylor turned around to go check on another guest. James grinned and asked Julia, "Would you like another drink before the movie?"

"Do you think I wouldn't?" Julia replied snarkily.

"Good point," he noted as he weaved his fingers with hers. They walked over to the bar in the courtyard, and after being served brandies, they found two seats. James held tightly to her hand as he asked her, "So do you and your fiance have time to go to the movies?"

"We get to go every once and awhile, but obviously this is a little bit fancier than what we normally get to do."

"Yeah, it's not often a movie star is sitting two rows ahead of you," James noted.

"I wonder which of her movies we are going to see?"

They each took a swill of their brandies before James responded, "I just hope it's not *Birth of a Nation*. Every time I see it, all I can think about is the whole movie is just one big line being fed to people. It's so historically inaccurate that I want to use the movie to manure my garden at home."

"I don't agree with the politics of it, but you have to admit it's a beautifully shot movie."

They both heard the organ beginning to pipe music around the house. Seeing the flicker of light beginning to shine, James leaned over and whispered, "I guess we are about to find out."

Sitting close and holding hands, the couple began to pay attention to the film, which was the actress's newest movie. As the plot unfolded, Julia steadily became more agitated, before she leaned over to James and whispered loudly, "I can't believe that man would ask her to leave her vows to the church."

"But he loves her and she loves him."

Julia frowned. "That doesn't matter. She promised herself to God and that's a vow you don't break! In fact, if anything ever happened to my fiance, I would probably do the same thing she did."

James looked at her dumbfounded. "So if something happened to him, you would seclude yourself from the world rather than try to find love again?"

"I would rather just find peace in seclusion."

James turned back to the movie, for some reason heartbroken at what she had just shared. Even though he was holding her hand, he felt further from her than he had since he first saw her on the platform in Jacksonville.

Chapter 12
The Letter

JAMES STARED STRAIGHT ahead as the movie ended with the nun asking God to keep her former lover safe until they meet again in heaven. Having decided during the course of the movie that tonight was a one time thing, he was silent as Julia began chattering about how wonderful the movie was and how happy she was the movie ended that way.

As they had held hands throughout the movie, Julia was startled when James pulled his hand from hers. He stood up and began to head to the table where drinks were being served, determined to have one more drink before Samuel was supposed to pick them up. He ordered a straight bourbon and downed it in one when he noticed Julia and Mr. Taylor coming to join him. James exhaled as Mr. Taylor spoke, "Dr. Pashen, Miss O'Connor, it has been a joy to have you here at Vizcaya for the night. I hope you will remember the night fondly."

Julia answered as she noticed the frown on James's face, "We will remember it forever."

James replied almost sarcastically, "Oh yes, WE will."

Taylor looked to each of them before answering, "Here is my business card," handing James and Julia each a card. "If you are ever in the area again, please let me know! I'd love to see you both." He then proceeded to shake James's hand and lightly kiss Julia's hand before walking toward the woman he had pointed out to James earlier in the evening.

Julia turned and stared at James, "What's wrong?"

"Nothing, Nothing at all. Let's go see if Samuel is here."

Julia frowned as James offered his arm instead of his hand, but rather than say anything, she put her hand on his elbow and they walked through the courtyard to the coat check. After receiving their coats, they walked out the front door and down the stairs toward the car.

Julia reached into her purse and pulled out her cigarette case, rubbing her thumb over the engraving. After pulling out a tool, she put her holder to her lips and lit the cigarette with her own lighter, not bothering to ask James. They waited for the cab, standing noiselessly next to each other. James was beginning to get slightly unsteady on his feet after shooting that last glass of bourbon, but continued his wall of silence as Julia kept glancing at him. Finally, Samuel cut through the awkwardness by calling for them through the window of the cab.

James opened the door to the cab to let Julia in before climbing in after her. This time he did not reach out to hold her hand but rather sat stone faced staring out the front windshield.

Samuel pushed the gas and they began to head back to the Flamingo. He glanced back at the couple and asked, "So how was the night?"

They answered in unison, "Fine."

Samuel was perplexed because most guests he had driven to Vizcaya left raving about the food, the drink, the mansion, the garden, or any other number of attractions the house held. He took a glance back at the pair before deciding that he was not going to get in the middle of whatever was happening. Samuel turned his focus to the road and remained mute.

Julia's confusion and anger continued to grow until she couldn't take it another minute. She turned toward James and hissed, "What has you in a lather?"

"What?" He responded coming out of his fog.

"I said, what had you in a lather?"

"Oh nothing. Don't worry about it."

"Don't worry about it! James, we were having a great night until that movie ended. Something happened to change that. What was it?"

"It's just...well," James stammered. "This can never be."

"What do you mean this can never be?"

Staring forward, James answered, "Julia, you are engaged to be married. I am married. Regardless of what we might feel, this can never be. And believe me, I feel a lot."

James turned and stared out his window, unable to articulate his feelings.

Julia placed a hand on his back and asked, "You feel a lot?"

James turned around and really beginning to feel the alcohol, replied, "Can you not feel this, this, this...thing between us? Something is here between us, and I know I can't be the only one who feels it."

Julia reached out and put her right hand on his left leg.

"James, no we don't have a future with each other. In a few days, we will go our separate ways and never see each other again. But we have right now. We have three days. We can have these three days together."

James glanced into her eyes and saw her sincerity. His head wobbled a little from the effects of the alcohol as he placed his hand on top of hers, but he did not reply.

Instead he turned and stared at the water as the car sped across the causeway toward Miami Beach and the Flamingo. The sliver of moonlight danced off the waves of the water as the reflection gave James a sense of inner peace. The taxi's engine hummed in his ears. Julia watched him expectantly, waiting for his answer.

After a few minutes, as the cab left the causeway and headed toward the hotel, Julia finally spoke.

"James?"

"Yes, Julia," he stated emphatically, still covering his hand on hers.

"What do you think? Could we spend the next three days together then go back to our regular lives?"

"That's what I meant by the yes," James smiled drunkenly.

Julia then moved close to him and kissed his cheek, curling her thin body against his. James's arm rested around her shoulders and pulled her close. He leaned down and kissed her head once, becoming enveloped in the coconut scent of her hair. He stared out the front windshield as the cab pulled into the hotel roundabout.

"Samuel," James said, handing him two dollars. "Thanks for the ride. Keep the change."

"Thank you, Mr. James!" Samuel exclaimed. Once Julia had left the cab and James was scooting out, Samuel added, "I hope the rest of the trip is great! But don't forget my advice."

James gaped at him before responding, "I think we both know it's too late for that, Samuel. Drive safely." James stepped out of the cab and inhaled the fresh night air. Taking out his pipe, he lit it before walking over to Julia who was standing under the awning. He took her hand and asked, "May I escort you to your room? I promise that's all I'll do tonight."

"Of course, I'd be honored," Julia smiled as they walked across the lobby to the elevator hand in hand.

"What floor?"

"Third, Room 301," Julia replied.

James stumbled slightly as they reached the elevator. "I'm on the third floor as well. 316."

"Are you sure I don't need to escort you? You are quite drunk by now."

James smiled goofily. "I'm fine. I can get much drunker."

"I'm sure you can!" Julia cracked.

They walked into the elevator when it opened, and James reached over and pushed the number three. He then pulled her close and smiled. "I really did have a wonderful night."

"So did I."

"What do you have planned for tomorrow?" James asked as the elevator rumbled to life and began to move.

"Well, I was going to go to a couple of speeches and some roundtables. What about you?"

"I don't have anything to do. Now that the speech is over, I have no set plans. Would you like to..." James was saying when the elevator doors opened.

They stepped out and headed down the dimly lit hall toward room 301. Julia held tightly to his arm.

When they arrived at her door, Julia turned and asked, "What were you going to say when the elevator opened?"

A goofy grin spread across his face. James asked, "Would you like to meet for brunch?"

"I would love to."

James beamed.

"Can we meet in the lobby at 9:30?" Julia asked. "Or will you be too hungover?"

"9:30 will be perfect."

James took her hand and brought it to his lips, lightly kissing it. He looked into her eyes and said enchantingly, "Goodnight, Miss O'Connor."

"Is that all I get?" She replied cheekily.

"If you remember correctly, I made you a promise not to kiss you tonight."

"Well then, I guess I'll just have to kiss you instead," she muttered before placing her hand on his cheek and initiating a kiss.

Closing his eyes, James savored the taste of her lips during the short kiss. Julia pulled away and smiled.

"Goodnight, James."

Julia opened the door and slipped inside the room.

James stood awestruck.

TAKING A SIP OF WATER, James finished his quick letter to Maude letting her know how the speech went and his opportunity to go to Vizcaya and meet William Taylor. He left out any mention of Julia, instead regaling Maude with the beauty and luxury evident throughout the mansion. Finishing up the letter, James put it in an envelope and placed it on the edge of the desk.

Still sitting at the desk, James looked down at the hotel stationary. On a whim, he decided to write Julia as well, knowing he would never send it.

January 7, 1924

My dearest Julia,

I can't believe it's only been 48 hours since I was dancing with you at Tobacco Road, holding you near me, looking into your eyes. Is this really my life? I'm not supposed to feel this way about anyone else but my wife, but after our conversation in the garden, you're all I seem to think about.

I know that it's impossible for you to feel the same way I do. I'm not sure anyone in the world can feel what I do. There's a chemistry between us that is unreal. But that's not the only thing that keeps drawing me. In just our few conversations, your passion for life, your turn of phrase, and your brain all make me want to be as close to you as I can for as long as I can.

Julia, I know you are promised to another as I am promised to Maude. Yet I can't stay away from you. Sometimes you just know something is right in this world, and that's how I see you. No one is perfect, obviously but you, you are just right. I don't know how else to explain it. I know you will never see this, so I will never have to explain it, but I already know. I love you. I love you with my whole being.

James stopped writing and just sat there, staring at the letter. He was overwhelmed with what he just wrote and what it all meant. Deciding to leave it unsigned, he place the letter back on top of the stationery and gulped down the rest of the water. Lying down, he immediately drifted off into a deep sleep.

Day 4
Tuesday, January 8, 1924

Chapter 13
The Brunch

A LIGHT WIND BLEW ACROSS Julia's face and hair as she tried to explain to James the history behind the Sistine Chapel as they walked around Vatican City.

"So the original art in the chapel was not Michelangelo's but rather Botticelli and a few others," Julia said.

Impulsively pulling her hand to his mouth, James kissed it lightly before they walked into the chapel and began to look up.

"I never realized the ceiling would be this low!" James said astounded.

"I know!" Julia responded. "When I was a child, I just assumed it was hundreds of feet in the air."

James began drinking in the paintings and after releasing Julia's hand, began to explore the chapel. He stared at the intricate marble floor before staring again at the ceiling. In awe, he simply stared until Julia walked up behind him and wrapped her arms around his stomach.

"This is incredible," James stated. "Thank you for sharing this with me."

She kissed his neck and whispered, "I'll make a Catholic out of you, yet."

The sun was shining brightly through the drapes on the window as James awoke with a smile plastered on his face. Rolling over onto his stomach and burying his head, James hoped to reenter the dream for a few more minutes. But the bliss of Rome with Julia had drifted away. James grunted into his pillow before glancing at the clock and seeing that he had over an hour until he was supposed to be in the lobby to meet Julia. After a few minutes, James flipped back over onto his back and put his hands behind his head. It was going to be a good day. Eventually, James swung his feet to the floor and headed to the shower.

JAMES DECIDED TO DRESS more casually for the brunch than he had for any other day in Miami. Wearing straight slacks and an open collared shirt, he approached the front desk for recommendations for brunch. The man at the front desk told him the only place in town that served a brunch better than the hotel was the Hibiscus Tea Room at the Burdine's department store in downtown Miami.

James thanked the desk worker before striding across the lobby to grab a morning paper. In his eagerness to see Julia, he actually had made it down to the lobby fifteen minutes early. After passing several flamingo statues, he sat down in a comfortable leather chair and propped his feet up before opening the front page. He placed his fedora on the end table next to the chair and began to read a story about Mexican rebels in the coastal town of Tampico. So engrossed he was in the newspaper, he did not see Julia walk up.

Wearing a maroon cloche hat with a matching skirt and white blouse, Julia smiled as she saw James deep in concentration while reading the newspaper. Julia glanced around the lobby to see that they were mostly alone since the convention had started for the day, so she decided to tease him just a bit. She circled around to the back of the chair and began to blow lightly on his neck. James shot up out of the chair like a cannonball, frightened as Julia burst into laughter at the sight of James's reaction. "Good morning!" Julia chimed jubilantly. "That reaction has already made my day complete!"

James scowled and said nothing for just a moment before he saw her smile. He couldn't be mad. "I guess my reaction was a bit funny."

"A bit!" Julia howled. "I may die from laughter if you have any worse reactions than that."

"Yeah, yeah," James muttered. At that point, he realized he hadn't fully looked at her today, and said as he gazed at her, "You look downright dishy in that hat."

"Well, thank you handsome," she smiled as she grabbed his hand. "So what fancy place are you taking me to this morning?"

"Well, the man at the desk recommended the Hibiscus Tea Room."

"Oh, I love tea!" Julia responded. "This is going to be a wonderful day." She leaned over and kissed his cheek. "So tell me what you were reading about?"

James began to explain the Mexican rebel story as she took his hand and led them out of the lobby. When they arrived at the cab, James opened the door for her and slid in behind her. "To Burdine's, please," James stated.

Still holding his hand, Julia said, "So what should we talk about this morning?"

Warmed by the feel of her hand, James thought for a moment before deciding to state, "Well I assume with the last name of O'Connor, you would come by your Catholicism honestly."

"Well, not quite," Julia beamed as genealogy was a passion of hers. "My father obviously comes from an Irish family, but my mother is originally from backwoods Kentucky, and before that, England. So religiously, my ancestors were half-Baptist, although my mother converted when she married my father."

"So how did they meet?" James asked intrigued. "After all, it's not exactly normal to have Irish immigrants in backwoods Kentucky."

"No, but there are lots in Cincinnati, and my mother had moved into the city to work in a bakery owned by our cousins. That's where she met Father. But I'm sure you have no interest in my childhood."

"Actually, I'd love to hear about it," James answered.

So as the car rambled across the causeway into downtown Miami, Julia began regaling him with stories about her childhood in Cincinnati and other parts of the midwest. Her dad was moved from fort to fort through his position in the U.S. Army. "... and there was even one year I lived in Alabama because of the danger where my dad was stationed near the Mexican border."

"Really? What part?"

"North Alabama, in a town called Guntersville," Julia answered before recalling a story of her childhood. James listened enraptured as she began talking about her sister Alice, and Alice's love of animals.

"... And then my mother was running out of the house, screaming at both Alice and me because we had let a prairie dog through the back door," Julia laughed. "I thought she would kill us that day."

"I'm glad to hear I wasn't the only one who infuriated their mother." James stuttered between breaths of laughter.

James leaned his head against the seat, looking at her. "It sounds like you had a wonderful childhood."

"I did, to be honest," Julia responded as the car stopped at the curb.

They stepped out of the cab and onto the sidewalk. Cars whizzed by as Julia grasped his hand. They looked up at the Burdine's sign that hung on the building. They entered the front door and began looking around the department store, taking in the sights of the displays. Eventually, they proceeded to the elevator and stepped in, heading for the canopied tea room.

AS THEIR BRUNCH OF tea sandwiches and lamb stew was being delivered, James was finishing a story about his daughter Abigail and her first doll. Julia was laughing at the appropriate places as she held her cigarette holder in her left hand. She reached to the ashtray and put out her cigarette before grabbing a sandwich and beginning to eat.

After a few bites, she put the sandwich down and took a sip of tea. Turning serious, she asked, "So what will you do now?"

"What do you mean?"

"Well, you're a little over 40, I'd guess."

"Under, thank you! I'm 38."

"Ok. 38. And with your speech yesterday, you have reached the pinnacle of your profession. What will you do now?"

James looked stumped. He grabbed his soda and drank. She was right, and he knew it because it was the same question he had been asking himself for weeks. His whole life had been focused on being accepted as a serious historian, and there was nothing more serious for a historian than to give a keynote speech at the AHA. Where did he go from here?

Julia watched him as his facial expressions changed. She knew he was deep in contemplation so she waited patiently for his answer. After collecting his thoughts James spoke, "What does one do when they have reached their goal?"

"Usually set a new one," she responded cheekily.

James rolled his eyes and responded, "Of course, but what would that be?"

"Well, I would assume that this would open up the possibility of looking at the most prestigious history positions in the country."

"But my family is happy in Charlottesville so looking for a new job is out of the question."

Julia pondered this and suggested, "Have you thought about writing? Or perhaps going on a speaking tour?"

"It's the research I've always loved much more than the writing," James replied.

They both turned back to the meal and began to eat in silence. James trying to think what he would do next with his life while Julia's thoughts began to grow darker. Eventually she looked up from her brunch and asked, "Am I just a diversion to keep your mind away from your impending malaise about life?"

"What?" James responded startled by her question.

"Here you are about to assess your life and decide what you need to change, and you just happen to fall for some young pretty girl because you have a few days away from real life. The way I see it, I am just a short diversion for you."

James looked at her confused by her remarks, "Where did that come from? In what way have I been insincere towards you?"

"You haven't been, but I just think you are spending time with me because I'm here and I'm available," Julia said dejectedly.

Affronted, James rasped, "You think I hit on women every time I'm away from my wife? You think this is normal for me?"

Julia spat back, "I don't know you at all!"

"Obviously!" James all but shouted as he stood up. He placed his napkin on the table and looked at Julia wearily. "I'm going to walk around the rooftop. I'll be back."

Walking away and breathing deeply, James walked to the edge of the rooftop canopy and looked out toward the ocean. Trying to calm himself, he took out his pipe and packed it with some Prince Albert tobacco. James lit the pipe and inhaled a deep breath of smoke. Was she right? Was his fascination with her due to the fact that his life had lost its meaning? Was she a diversion that was keeping him away from thinking about how he had no real direction in life now that the speech was over?

He brought the pipe to his lips and took another deep drag. Pipe in his right hand, James leaned his elbows and looked out toward the Atlantic Ocean. Lost in his own thoughts, he did not hear Julia approach from behind and lean over next to him. "I am sorry about earlier," she said soothingly. "I know this has to be a difficult time for you, and whatever capacity you need, I am here for the next few days."

James turned his head toward her. Noticing her cigarette unlit, he silently pulled his lighter from his right pocket and lit her cigarette. His eyes moved back to the ocean and he lost himself in the movement of the waves as they both silently smoked. Still looking away, James eventually responded, "Julia, I don't know what is happening or why, but I know that you're the person I want to share this moment with. Can that be enough for you?"

A simple "Yes" was all that came from her mouth.

Chapter 14
The Suit

AN HOUR LATER, THE mood was still subdued as the cab meandered across the causeway back to the Flamingo. The weather outside fit the mood as there was a light rain belting the windshield of the yellow cab. Julia's question still stuck in his head, and he couldn't figure out the answer. What would he do with the rest of his life?

Julia, having decided that James had been thinking long enough, chimed in with a false whine in her voice, "Do we really have to go to meetings this afternoon?"

James was pulled out of his brooding. "What do you mean?"

"Well, we have only a few days more here in Miami with each other. Surely we can find something better to do that go to hear a talk on the importance of Versailles to the reign of Louis the XIV!" Julia smiled mischievously.

"Well what did you have in mind?" James smiled and took her hand.

Smiling as she felt his caress on the back of her hand, Julia responded, "Would you like to go to the beach?"

James looked out of the side window of the cab and asked, "Do you think the weather is going to clear up?"

The driver, who had been eavesdropping, chimed in, "Miami storms pop up all the time. This one will be gone within the hour."

Julia beamed as James looked at her and said, "It would make sense to go at least once while we are here. I'd love to."

"Do you have a bathing suit?"

"No, we might need to procure one of those."

Julia responded, happy with herself that she was right in thinking James did not bring a bathing suit, "Well we can ask the desk attendant at the hotel where we should go to find one." She kissed his cheek at the same time the cab stopped in the hotel drive.

After James paid the cabbie, they climbed out of the cab. As James headed to the front desk to ask where the best place to buy swimwear was, Julia began to ascend the stairs in the corner of the lobby. She called out to James, "I'll be back down in a few minutes!"

James watched her climb the stairs in admiration before turning to the desk manager. "Where can I go to buy a bathing suit?"

"Well, there are several places on the island, but if you go to one of the casinos, you can simply rent a suit for the day," the manager suggested.

"Um, no thanks, I'd prefer to buy," James noted as he glanced around the lobby and saw Walter.

The desk manager cleared his throat to get James's attention again. "Well there are a few stores opening up on Lincoln Road, but at this time of year, the water will be pretty chilly."

James nodded in agreement before replied, "True, but when the woman wants to go to the beach, you go to the beach."

"Yes sir, I can agree with that."

James slipped him a dollar and shook his hand, "Thanks for the help!"

James then turned around and looked for Walter to go say hello to him when he saw him standing close to Dr. Fallon. She was touching his arm lightly while sporting a glowing smile. So instead of interrupting the tender moment, James walked back to the same leather chair he was sitting in that morning.

He grabbed a Time Magazine that was left on the table and found an article on lynchings in the South. Since it related somewhat to his field of study, he became engrossed in the aspects of the story.

Julia stepped off the last step to enter the lobby when she saw him in the same chair as earlier, the back of his head bent down in concentration as he read. She slowly walked up behind him and just decided to watch him for a minute. She quickly noticed the graying hair around his temples and the way that his glasses laid crookedly across his ears. And yet he looked relaxed as he read. A sense of peace and contentment washed over her, and she knew that for that moment, there was no other place in the world she'd rather be.

She moved closer hoping to catch a glimpse of what he was reading. Close enough to reach out and touch him, she saw the article on lynching and realized that through all the craziness of the past few days, this man before her would be a part of her always. Instinctively, she placed her hand on his shoulder and looked down at him.

James gazed into her hazel eyes. Lost for a moment, he smiled naturally. Her dark curls flowed down her face as she looked down at him. He thought she had never looked more beautiful. He placed his hand on top of hers in silent understanding.

James stood and noticed a leather shopping bag around her shoulder. He assumed it held her swimsuit. "We will be taking a cab to Lincoln Road, where there should be a store for me to find some type of swimsuit to wear."

She took his hand in hers and said, "Sounds good to me!"

As they walked to the door, James began to tell her what he saw between Walter and Jeanette. Enjoying the gossip, Julia asked if he thought Walter and Jeanette had noticed them. Thinking for a second, he stated that the two were so lost in themselves that there was no way they saw either James or Julia.

She then smiled and kissed his cheek as they walked outside to the bright sun shining after the rain, "I don't think I've told you this yet, but the beach is my favorite place in the world! The ocean and I are one with each other."

"Then I'm happy to share this experience with you. However, I have to warn you, the water is going to be cold."

"You forget I live in Chicago, this water will be like a bathhouse to me," Julia joked.

ON LINCOLN ROAD, THEY continued to walk hand-in-hand as they looked for a store selling men's bathing wear.

"So do you have any preference on a bathing suit?" Julia asked as they looked into a shop window filled with books.

"Well, I have to admit I've never owned one."

"What?" Julia said incredulously.

"I've never owned a bathing suit." James responded shrugging his shoulders.

"But why not? Going to the beach and getting into the water is the most wonderful feeling in the world!" Julia exclaimed.

"Well, I've never lived near a beach. My wife's family lives in the mountains, and frankly, when swimming, we often are alone and don't need bathing clothes," James shrugged.

Julia bent over laughing, removing her hand from James's in the process. "So you don't wear clothes when you swim?"

"Well, I grew up on a farm, and we just swam in the pond. However, it's been a long time since I went swimming," he grinned at her mirth. As they walked further down the row of shops, Julia spotted a men's store. Pointing to the door, she proposed, "Why don't we see what's available here?"

James looked apprehensive as they walked into the store. Shelves lined the walls of the store, and each shelf was filled with folded clothes. When he spotted the swimsuits, he began to blush when he saw the suits they had available. Noticing, Julia poked him in the side and said, "Don't be a bluehose. This will be fun!"

Acquiescing to her desires, James allowed her to lead him to the counter, where she spoke up, "Hello sir! My fella here is in the market for a bathing suit. Could you show us what might work well for him?"

"Sure miss, what did you two have in mind?"

"Something comfortable for this beautiful January day," Julia responded enthusiastically as she pulled on James's hand slightly.

"I have just the thing," the shopkeeper said as he led them to a shelf of clothes near the back of the store. He pointed and noted, "These here look about your size, sir."

Julia thanked the shopkeeper before beginning to look through the bathing suits, looking for the one she thought would look best on James. She would pick one up and let it unfold before staring at the suit then back at James. She did this several times when James began to get a bit antsy. She walked up to him and kissed his cheek before handing him two bathing suits. "Go try these on," she ordered. James took the two suits and silently walked to the fitting room, examining the choices she made.

After pulling the curtain behind him, James looked closely at the suits. The first was a deep cut wool tank top that would cling to his body down his chest to the top of his legs, with a pair of shorts to go with it. Black with three white stripes at the bottom of the shirt, James had never worn anything this revealing outside of his home in his entire life. The second suit was similar in style but colored in dark blue. Deciding that he did not want to disappoint Julia, he began to undress to put the blue one on.

When finished, James looked in the mirror and was horror-struck. Not only had he never worn anything so revealing, he also had never worn anything so tight. And being almost 40, he wasn't sure that Julia would find him attractive once she saw him in this. He sat on the stool in the fitting room, trying to get the courage to get up and show her. He was spurred on by her voice. "Let me see!" she practically squealed.

Still hesitant, James responded warily, "I'm not so sure about this."

"James Pashen, either you step out here, or I'm coming in there! And believe me, I will make a scene about coming in!" Julia demanded.

With a huff, James stood and opened the curtain. Julia looked him up and down before smiling, "I thought that would look perfect on you!"

James rolled his eyes. "I'm sure your fiance would look much better in this."

"Who am I here with?"

"Me," James said sheepishly.

"And I wouldn't want it any other way." Julia smiled.

James nodded conceding the point.

"Ok then. So do you prefer the blue or the black?" Julia asked.

"Definitely the blue."

"Then go back in there and change and we will buy these." She reached out and grabbed the two straps of the tank top and pulled him in for a quick kiss.

Beaming, James backed up and pulled the curtain to the dressing room.

FORTY FIVE MINUTES later, they stepped out of a cab and through the front doors of the Fisher's St. John's Casino, a bath house with pools and beach access. Julia placed her hand on James's elbow and in her excitement, almost dragged him to the front desk. A faint smell of flowery tobacco mixed with the salt air as a young woman with a short bob haircut welcomed them to the casino. After a quick exchange, she handed James a key and two fluffy towels before directing the couple to their cabana for the afternoon.

They followed the young woman's directions, which took them down a hall before ascending a flight of stairs to their room. Julia was almost giddy with excitement as James opened the door. They stepped into a standard looking hotel room with a bathroom connected to it. As she walked toward the bed, Julia chimed in, "Do you want the bathroom or the bedroom to change?"

"Are you really that eager to get to the beach?" James questioned.

"Have you been paying attention to me at all the last two hours? Of course, I want to go to the beach now!"

James chuckled and responded, "Alright, alright. I'll take the bathroom." He grabbed his new bathing suit and headed to the bathroom. Just before leaving the room, he turned to smile at her, but she had already gone over to her bag and began to get her suit out. Being a gentleman, he turned back around and walked through the bathroom door, shutting it behind him.

James looked into the mirror. Staring at himself, he realized it was the first time he had stopped since brunch a few hours earlier. The melancholy began to set in once again now mixed with some guilt. What would he do with the rest of his life? And why was he doing something that would hurt Maude so much?

He placed his hands on the counter and leaned toward the mirror. He began to think back on his life, on his childhood on the farm, on his schooling at API, on his life with Maude and on his career at Virginia.

Looking into his own eyes, he began to ask himself. Who was he? How did he get here? What led him to be in this cabana with a 21 year old student from Chicago?

"James!" Julia called from the other side of the door. "I'm ready to go whenever you are!"

Hearing the excitement in her voice, James decided he'd revisit those thoughts later. "Give me just a moment, and I'll be out!"

Chapter 15
The Beach

JULIA STOOD LOOKING out the window, tapping her feet as she waited. Puffing gently on her cigarette, she was impatient to be on the beach seeing as it had been the summer before since she had gotten into the water. She finished up her cigarette and put it into the ashtray when the bathroom door opened.

Dressed in his blue bathing suit, James opened the bathroom door and was stunned still. Julia looked like Persephone, a beautiful maiden just out of his reach. And for a moment, James considered whether he should become her Hades and steal her away. Pushing the ridiculous thought from his mind, he simply stared instead. Julia was adorned in a maroon Jantzen suit that clung to her petite body. Reflexively, he looked down at her bare legs and stared at her well-defined calves, obviously sculpted by lots of dancing. By this point, James had forgotten about his troubled thoughts, and instead tried to take a mental picture in his head of her standing there next to the window. He had never seen a woman so beautiful and wanted to never forget that moment.

As he was drinking in her appearance, Julia turned and saw him. She smirked as she knew he was mesmerized. She tilted her head silently questioning him.

He grinned goofily at her before she beckoned him over with a curl of her finger. His eyes spoke of a hunger for her as he crossed the small room in two steps. He pulled her close and whispered into her ear, "You look bewitching."

She quipped as she placed her palms on his chest, "Are you sure the spell is working? I was beginning to worry that you were about to climb out the bathroom window and leave me here alone."

"Well, I thought about it, but we are on the second floor, and my joints can't take that kind of jump anymore," James jokingly shrugged. "So I decided I just would put up with you for a little while longer."

Julia pulled away in a false huff and punched him in the arm.

"Hey now! I'm old!" James exclaimed.

"Oh hush it! Let's go to the beach!"

Julia grabbed his hand and began to lead him out of the cabana when James stopped her and kissed her for a long moment. Pulling away, Julia mouthed "Later." As they walked by the bed James grabbed both towels and the room key and they headed down to the beach.

JULIA SPLASHED IN THE water as the waves came lazily toward the beach. Looking like a peaceful mermaid who had finally found water again, James could not help but be affected by her display of pure joy. Although he was standing 30 feet away on the edge of the cool water and could hear conversations behind him, it seemed to him as if they were the only two people on the beach.

"Come join me!" Julia called out to James.

"I'm good here thanks! Besides the view is pretty spectacular!"

Her eyebrows arched. "Are you talking about me or the ocean?"

"Which do you think?"

Julia pondered this for a moment as she walked back toward the shore and James. "Well, the ocean is beautiful and there are several hotsy-totsy women here today." She pointed toward the beach and waved her hand.

James looked at her for a short time before quickly picking her up and laying her over his shoulder. He growled, "Have I taken my eyes off of you at all in the last three days?"

"Put me down!" Julia yelped.

"I grow tired of your insolence," James rebuked as he walked a few steps in the ocean before throwing Julia into the water, drenching her from head to foot.

James stood above her smiling when she grabbed his ankle and yanked him down as well. "Now we are even!" she said grinning as she scooted next to him and kissed his cheek. Sitting beside him in the water, she stated, "You know there is no place in the world I love more than the beach. In fact, if I was a Greek goddess I would have been Aphrodite."

"Aphrodite, huh?" James responded thoughtfully. "I saw you more as a Persephone."

Curious, Julia asked, "Really? How come?"

James, keen to avoid that subject, decided to state instead, "I've never really thought about which god I would have been."

"You'd have been Hephaestus."

"Isn't that the same as Vulcan, god of the forge?"

"Yes it is," Julia replied.

"I don't see that comparison."

Julia smirked mischievously and said, "Well, like you, Vulcan has no pants and has a nice round ass."

James turned beet red at her statement as she splashed him in the face. She jumped up and ran back to the deeper waves, this time with James on her heels, both of them laughing joyously. When he caught up with her, he tried to dunk her into the water, but she was too quick and got behind him and held on for dear life.

"Stop! Stop!" She bantered while James tried to reach behind him and grab her. "Stop! I have to tell you something."

James stopped reluctantly and said, "And what do you have to tell me that is so important?

"So you know how a few minutes ago, you didn't want to get in?"

"Yes, what about it?"

"I won," Julia declared triumphantly.

"What do you mean, you won?"

"Look where you are. I won. You're out here with me and not some fraidy-cat on the shore. I. Won." Julia laughed and stuck out her tongue.

James looked at her incredulously before snatching her and throwing her into the water one more time. He then announced with a broad smile, "I concede."

He reached out and clasped her hand. Pulling her into a hug, he muttered quietly, "Thank you for winning."

"Anytime! I like to win and I really don't like to lose," Julia responded with a kiss on James's cheek.

"I'll remember that," was all James could say as they held each other and looked out upon the ocean.

"I TOOK TO THE WATER from the time I was born," Julia told him as they lounged next to each other on the beach, laying twenty yards from the windmill that powered the water to the pools. Propped up on her left elbow, Julia continued the story, "My father was stationed in Texas when I was born, and we went down to the ocean when I was about a year old. Now obviously I have no recollection of this, but my mother swears the first time I was placed in the water, a wave knocked me over. She was about to panic when she saw my face. I was giggling uncontrollably. That's when my family knew I was made for the water."

The winter sun warmed them as James, propped up on his right elbow, responded, "So how often do you get to the beach?"

"Well in the summer, I get to go fairly often since there is a beach just off Lake Michigan; however, I haven't been to the ocean in three years. My family went to Atlantic City back in '21."

"Fun fact, I've never been north of the Mason-Dixon Line," James noted when he began to think about Atlantic City.

"Oh really? Because of my dad's work in the army, I've been nearly everywhere in the U.S. and have been to Europe twice."

Thinking back to the dream from the morning, James gazed off into the distance before stating, "Well, I'm envious. I've always wanted to go to Europe."

Julia looked at him tenderly for just a moment before stating, "Ok, your turn. Tell me something about your childhood."

James chuckled, "You've already heard the shotgun story, so let me think."

"Make it good!"

"Ok, so as you can guess with a brother only eighteen months younger than me, Harold and I were often getting into all sorts of scrapes. Perhaps the second worse whipping I ever received was for my antics at a local church gathering. Our church was having a picnic after church in late May, and it's really hot in Eufaula in late May, so my brother and I got the bright idea to go to the water pump that was outside the church and cool ourselves off."

Julia interjected at this point, "So how old were you two then?" as her hand lightly laid on his side.

"I must have been ten which would have made Harold nine."

"OK. Continue."

"So anyways, we start pumping water and taking turns sticking our heads under the pump. Understand that this is right after church on Sunday so we are in the best set of clothes we have at the time. So we are soaked but feeling pretty good about ourselves because we aren't sweltering hot anymore. However, I made a fatal error. I decided to trip Harold for the fun of it. He fell over and into the dirt, which of course stuck to him because he was all wet. So he ran after me and when he caught me pushed me down into the dirt as well. Next thing you know, we are wrestling each other in our finest church clothes in front of the entire congregation. I thought my father was going to kill us and dump us in the Chattahoochee!"

Julia was laughing by the end of the story, when she asked, "Did you like living in one place when you were young?"

James thought for a moment before answering, "I think I appreciate it more now than I did as a child. When everything in the world goes to shit, you have a place to go home to. Eufaula is that place for me. Harold still runs the family business."

Julia said thoughtfully, "I wish I had a place like that."

They stared at each other sympathetically before Julia asked, "Do you have any plans for dinner?"

"I had hoped I would be spending it with you."

"Good, because I'm hungry."

James stood up and reached out his hand. She took it.

Chapter 16
The Date

"WELCOME TO JOE'S DINER!" a plump old lady chimed as the couple walked into the restaurant. "Will it be just you two dining with us this evening?"

"Yes, ma'am," James said politely, with Julia's left hand on his right arm.

"I see you two are engaged," the lady smile brightly, noticing the ring on Julia's finger. "When is the big day?"

"Yes, dear, when IS the big day?" James responded, realizing that he had no idea when she was getting married. At the same time, he subtly put his left hand in the pocket of his brown suit pants, hoping the nice lady did not notice his ring.

Julia, dressed in a simple black dress, looked up at James curiously before playing along, "We are getting married in two weeks, on the 19th of this month."

"Oh so soon!" the woman said excitedly. "I love weddings! Let me give y'all our best table. Well, our second best table. Our best table is currently occupied."

"Lead the way," Julia chimed.

The couple followed in amusement as the woman led them to a nice corner table on the glass patio. Nearly every table was filled and conversations filled the air. The lady pointed to a white clothed table, and after pouring them each a water, began to tell the couple about the specials available. She especially raved about the stone crab. After finishing her speil, she walked away to the kitchen and James and Julia looked at each other and burst into laughter.

"So two weeks huh?" James asked still trying to stop laughing.

"Yes, Albert and I are getting married in two weeks," Julia said nonchalantly before changing the subject. "So are you still going to try the stone crab?"

"When in Miami, we should eat as Miamians eat," James said then took a sip of his water.

"Good plan, except I don't enjoy seafood."

"You don't enjoy seafood?" James asked incredulously.

"Why does everyone react that way when I say that?"

"Because seafood is wonderful, especially when it is prepared right. And since this is the best place on the island to get it, I would assume this would be especially great. You should have told me that you didn't like seafood before I brought you here."

"Well the guy at the desk said they make a great steak so I decided not to say anything. Besides, I knew you were excited about eating here and trying the stone crab," Julia spoke as she reached across the table and grabbed his hand. Their eyes met for a moment before being interrupted.

The server, who introduced herself as Jennie, came back to the table, placing down a tea for Julia and a soda for James, and took their order. After gushing over them for another moment, Jennie headed toward the kitchen to put in their orders.

James held her hand tightly and asked, "So we've talked about my future or lack thereof, what are your long term plans?"

"Well, I have a semester left at the University of Chicago before I will go to graduate school. I hope to go and study with Dr. Fallon at Barnard College. Speaking of Dr. Fallon, I don't think you're the only man who has fallen for someone this week."

"Well, Walter seems to always be after some woman, but he actually seems to be truly interested in Jeanette. But anyway, please continue."

"Well, if I don't go there, I will continue to study under Dr. Grossman in Chicago. A lot depends on if Albert can find a job in New York."

James nodded before continuing, "Now I remember you mentioning something about chemistry before, but what does he want to do with that degree?"

"Actually he is already a pharmacist. He graduated a year ago. Albert has a good job now in Chicago, but I really want to go to school in New York."

"Understandable, Dr. Fallon is one of the preeminent historians in the country. Hopefully Albert will be able to find a job that will allow you to do that," James said honestly.

Julia smiled and replied, "My long term hope is to be able to work at historical biblical sites, doing archeological work."

"I'm impressed. Sounds like you have it all figured out."

"Well, that's the plan anyway, but God may change that at any time."

James nodded in agreement, "Yes he may."

Julia excused herself for a moment and placed her napkin on the table. James sat and began to stare out the window. Walking by the restaurant was an older couple holding hands and laughing with each other. This led James back to thinking once again on his own future. He grabbed his flask from his pocket and took a deep swig of rum while waiting for Julia to come back to the table. He realized that he only had one more full day in Miami, and had not even thought to ask Julia if she was leaving tomorrow or Thursday. The reality of the entire situation began to overwhelm him. His future, his wife and family at home, his falling for Julia, and his life overall confounded him and the look on his face slowly turned sour and a faint sense of guilt began to pervade.

It was in that moment that Jennie shuffled to the table with their food. She looked at James's expression and asked, "Everything alright, honey?"

"What?" James answered. "Oh sorry, I'm just thinking too much."

"Well, let me tell you something I noticed about that Jane you're with. She absolutely adores you. You can see it in her eyes. Now I don't know what all issues you have, especially since I see that ring you have on."

James quickly interceded, "I'm sorry. We shouldn't have acted like we were engaged."

Jennie gave him a grandmotherly look. "It's ok honey. You both seem to be sweet people. But I'm telling you now, whatever is going on, don't be a killjoy tonight. Take it from someone who has seen lots of couples come through those doors over the years, it's unreal how she looks at you. So don't be a spoilsport! Give her a wonderful night." Jennie stopped the short lecture as she saw returning to the table.

In a loud voice, she said, "I hope you enjoy your dinner!" before turning away and checking on another table.

James contemplated what she said as he watched her walk away. Julia arrived at the table and looked questioningly at James.

"What was that about?" Julia queried.

"She was giving me a bit of advice."

"Why?"

"Because she's wiser than I am," James said jokingly before beginning to peel the first stone crab claw.

JAMES PEELED BACK THE shell of another stone crab and dipped it into melted butter before taking a bite. The savory flavor caused him to let out an audible sigh of pleasure as he avidly dipped the crab meat again. "So how is your steak?" he asked Julia.

"Delectable," she responded brightly, stabbing it with a fork and cutting another piece.

"Since I picked the restaurant, would you like to choose the next part of the evening?" James said while taking a sip of his soda.

"What are my choices?"

James responded, "Well, there's a place not far from here that the hotel manager told me had some gambling, especially roulette wheels. Or we could go back to the Flamingo and dance for a while."

"Oh that's easy, I want to go dancing!" Julia exclaimed as she reached over and stole some of James's hash browns.

"Ok. Well, you may have to help me out. I can do slower dances, but I'm not exactly up to date on some of the more exciting dances that are now in fad."

"Well then, I hope you are as good a student as you are a teacher," Julia winked. "This will be so much fun!"

As he peeled another crab, James said, "As long as you promise not to laugh at me too much, we should have a good time."

"Well, if it will help you, I found out from Dr. Grossman that the Flamingo serves alcohol if you ask the right people, so perhaps we can get you a little something to help loosen you up, and not be such a pill," Julia ribbed.

"So you just see me as this 'Father Time,' huh?" James asked as he grabbed his soda.

Julia raised her eyebrows and joked, "Not a 'Father Time' but maybe a daddy."

James nearly spit out his drink before staring into her beautiful eyes. He was dumbstruck by her innuendo when she burst out laughing. "You should have seen your face!" She howled. "I thought you were going to jump across this table and take me right here and now."

"I thought about it," James fired back.

Julia looked at him contemplating the exchange before deciding to change the subject. "I can't wait to teach you all the latest dances," Julia declared beaming.

"Again, fair warning, I am a terrible dancer."

"Maybe you just haven't had the right partner."

"I can't wait to find out if you are right."

Julia quipped, "I usually am."

"JAMES! YOU ARE NOT listening to me!" Julia said exasperatedly.

"I told you I couldn't dance!" James huffed back.

"Let's try again," Julia said as she walked him through the basic steps of the foxtrot. "Now as I move my foot forward, you will move your foot back like so."

Finally getting the first couple of steps right, Julia kissed his cheek while the band continued to play "Felix the Cat" in the background. "I think you are starting to get this!"

James beamed, "Well we can either praise your wonderful teaching or the copious amounts of alcohol I've already taken in."

"You haven't had that much."

"I suppose you are right but I'm going to need more if I'm going to keep this up," James noted.

"Well, you better keep drinking because I want to keep dancing with you."

The squeaks of shoes on the hardwood floor enveloped the room full of dancers as the jazz band played in the background. Smoke clung to the ceiling as those watching the dancers enjoyed their evening.

As the song ended, the dancers clapped before the band began a rousing rendition of "Somebody Stole My Gal."

Julia chuckled, "Well that's just screwy for them to play this song next." She winked. "Let's go get another drink."

She grabbed his elbow as they made their way from the dance floor to find the correct waiter who was bringing the booze. When they located him, James asked, "Could the lady and I have the house giggle-water?"

He smiled and responded, "Of course."

James whispered to him, "Make mine a double."

Julia heard him and asked, "Are you sure you need that much?"

"To keep dancing with you, maybe not, but to keep my brain at bay, most definitely."

"What's bothering you?"

James looked into her eyes and barely held it together. "I think the better question is what isn't bothering me."

"What do you mean?"

James took a deep breath and was about to speak when the tuxedoed waiter brought back their drinks. James paid for the drinks and tipped him handsomely before turning back to Julia.

James looked far away as he thought to himself, *Where do I begin? In my professional life, I have nowhere to go but down. In my personal life, I am married to this peach of a woman who's always supported me even when life has become monotonous and yet at the same time, I've met this amazing and wonderful woman who will leave me in a day or two and go marry someone else. Then there is this growing sense of guilt that I know I am choosing to defy everything I believe, and yet I can't stop. And that doesn't even start getting into everything else. The only things holding me together tonight are you and the hooch.*

He finally looked into Julia's mesmerizing eyes. He took a deep swig of his drink. On the verge of tears, he took a deep breath and extended his hand. "May I have the next dance?"

Chapter 17
The Drunk

JAMES STUMBLED OVER the dance steps again as the band continued a jittery edition of "Love Will Find a Way." Julia rolled her eyes but held onto his hand and shoulder.

Knowing that James had drank a lot of alcohol, Julia suggested, "Why don't we sit down and rest a bit."

"That might be a good idea," James slurred slightly, his eyes red from the amount of drink he had.

Julia grabbed his elbow lightly and began to lead him back to their table on the side of the dance floor. He swayed slightly as they walked, unsteady on his feet after a couple of hours of dancing and a lot of alcohol along the way.

"You're really pretty," James muttered as he smiled drunkenly at her. "Have I told you that before?"

"A few times in the last hour, yes," Julia snickered. "The term giggle water certainly applies to you tonight."

James drunkenly laughed, "It does, doesn't it."

Julia gave him an indulgent smile. "Are you sure you don't need to go up to bed? You are having a hard time standing up."

"I know, but if I go to bed now, I lose precious time with you that will soon be at an end." James said morosely. "I want to be around you for as long as I can."

"Point taken," Julia noted.

As they arrived back at the high round table, Julia tried to reach and grab James's drink before he could but he noticed and frowned slightly, "So you're not going to let me have anymore? So you're going to be my alarm clock now?"

Firing up, Julia responded, "Someone's got to take care of you, and it's obvious you're not doing it yourself."

"Don't be a canceled stamp! It doesn't become you." James fired back, hoping to get more alcohol.

"James, you can barely stand, and I won't have you passing out in here. You are cut off."

She looked sternly at him. "I'm so sorry I called you a papist." James said sincerely. He laid his chin on his arm and looked at Julia with puppy dog eyes.

"That's it! I'm taking you to bed."

"What?" James responded alarmed. "I didn't realize we had decided to do that."

Julia blushed slightly but rolled her eyes. "Not that kind of taking you to bed. It's time you went to sleep. Come on my fella, let's get you upstairs."

James looked at her unsure for a moment before deciding she was right, and it was time for him to lay down. He swayed a bit while pushing away from the table before Julia came over, held his elbow and helped him slowly to the elevator.

They were completely focused on each other as James looked at her and smiled. "You have really pretty eyes. Did you know that?"

Julia giggled a little before responding, "You are a very flirty drunk."

"Am I?" James said self-consciously as he almost tripped into the elevator. "I can stop. Do you want me to stop?"

"No. It's all right. This is certainly much better than you being a mean or violent drunk."

James nodded, "You are correct again, ma'am."

Holding onto her for dear life, James and Julia got into the elevator. As the elevator door closed and Julia pushed the three button, James leaned on the wall of the elevator. He turned toward her and mumbled, "My room is 316. Wait, how did you know I was staying on the third floor?"

"Because you told me last night, you goof," Julia commented. "You are really forgetting things aren't you?"

"I hope I don't forget you," James said worriedly. "I think I'd be very sad in the morning if you were just a dream."

The elevator dinged as Julia leaned in, and touching his cheek she kissed him once. "Hopefully you'll remember me in the morning."

As the door opened, James gestured wildly with his hand and slurred, "My room is thataway." Julia watched amused as he tried to stumble himself down the hall to his room. Eventually she put him out of his misery and grabbed his elbow.

"This way, my fella."

"I'M SO SORRY I GOT so blotto," James mumbled almost incoherently as he laid face down on his bed, still on top of the covers.

Silently, Julia was attentive to the waves crashing into the shore as she removed his coat and shoes and placed them in the closet. She walked back to the bed and just stared for a long moment at him laying face down into the pillow.

Eventually, she sat beside him and played with his hair. "I'm just glad I'm here to make sure you are ok." After lightly caressing his scalp for several minutes in silence, Julia realized he was about to fall asleep so she ordered, "Now climb under the covers."

James obediently got under the covers before exclaiming, "You're so wonderful. Albert must be an amazing guy to get to deserve you."

"I think I am the lucky one, because I don't think I deserve him," she responded honestly.

James turned his head toward her. "Well I'm so glad you have someone who loves you and you love. You deserve it." He smiled drunkenly. "I'm going to sleep now."

Julia continued to sit on the edge of the bed, lightly touching his back as he immediately dropped off to sleep. Eventually she leaned down and pushed the hair off his forehead before laying a light kiss on it.

She realized that he would wake up in the morning and likely forget most of the last part of the night, so she decided to write him a note explaining why he was sleeping in his suit, as well as retelling the story of what happened before he went to sleep. Slowly standing up from the bed, she tiptoed over to the desk.

When she got to the desk, she grabbed the top piece of stationary and grabbed a pen. When she looked down to the paper, she noticed writing on it and began to read.

January 7, 1924

My dearest Julia,

I can't believe it's only been 48 hours since I was dancing with you at Tobacco Road, holding you near me, looking into your eyes. Is this really my life? I'm not supposed to feel this way about anyone else but my wife, but after our conversation in the garden, you're all I seem to think about.

I know that it's impossible for you to feel the same way I do. I'm not sure anyone in the world can feel what I do. There's a chemistry between us that is unreal. But that's not the only thing that keeps drawing me. In just our few conversations, your passion for life, your turn of phrase, and your brain all make me want to be as close to you as I can for as long as I can.

Julia, I know you are promised to another as I am promised to Maude. Yet I can't stay away from you. Sometimes you just know something is right in this world, and that's how I see you. No one is perfect, obviously but you, you are just right. I don't know how else to explain it. I know you will never see this, so I will never have to explain it, but I already know. I love you. I love you with my whole being.

Julia leaned back, stunned at what she had read. She glanced over to where James was sleeping peacefully on his stomach. How could he write such a thing? She leaned toward the desk and began to read the letter again. Certain phrases kept jumping out at her. *My dearest Julia... you're all I seem to think about... I'm not sure anyone in the world can feel what I do... you are just right... I love you with my whole being.*

Overwhelmed, Julia's eyes began darting around the room when she saw James's flask at rest on top of the dresser. She walked over quietly and grabbed the flask. After taking a swill which warmed her, she shuffled slowly back to the desk, taking the flask with her. She sat down and began sipping on the rum, trying to decide what to do. Leaning back in the chair, she looked at the ceiling and silently prayed, "Ave Maria, gratia plena, Dominus tecum. Benedicta tu in mulieribus, et benedictus fructus ventris tui, Iesus. Sancta Maria, Mater Dei, ora pro nobis peccatoribus, nunc, et in hora mortis nostrae. Amen."

She didn't know what to think or do. Should she proceed with her original plan and leave a note for James? Should she just leave the room? And how did she feel about what she read? What did this mean about tomorrow? About going home?

Taking a few more sips of rum, she decided she needed to think on what she read. Julia stood up slowly and quietly left the room.

As she slowly shut the door, James was snoring in the background.

Day 5
Wednesday, January 9, 1924

Chapter 18
The Confrontation

THE POUNDING IN JAMES'S head grew louder as he tried to cover his ears.

"Go away," he mumbled into his sheet when Walter burst through the door.

"Where the hell have you been?" Walter practically shouted as he ripped open the curtains.

Covering his head with his arms, James pleaded, "Please not so loud."

"You look bent."

"I still feel bent."

Walter strode to the bathroom and filled up a glass with water. He brought it to James who squinted as he sat up a bit and began to sip the water.

"Here, take this," Walter said, handing James a couple of aspirin.

"Thanks," James whispered.

Walter sat down in the chair opposite the bed and just stared at James for several minutes as James struggled with his hangover. Scanning the room, Walter noticed the breeze whipping through the window when his eyes fell on a piece of paper on the desk. Walter was about to get up and look at it when James began to move. So Walter resumed the conversation, "So how much did you have?"

James, with his eyes still closed as he sat up, answered, "I lost count somewhere around eight or nine."

"And I assume Julia was impressed by all this?"

"What?"

"Well I assume she was with you all day," Walter started with his bushy eyebrows raised. "Neither Ira nor I saw either of you until late last night when you were stumbling across the lobby."

"You saw?" James asked concerned.

"You were kind of hard to miss."

"Was I really that bad?"

Walter sniggered, "I'll put it this way. I'd avoid Ira today if I was you."

James rubbed his eyes a bit before responding, "Why? I thought Ira knew about my situation with Julia and was ok with it."

"Maybe once he saw how into each other you were last night, he became concerned again. Either way, he isn't happy with either of you, but especially you."

James pondered this statement as he sat on the edge of the bed. "Well that's good to know. What time is it?" James asked as he squinted toward the clock.

Walter looked down at his watch before responding, "8:06."

James looked angry. "Why did you wake me up so early? My head is splitting open."

"And that's your own fault. You can't miss another day of the conference. People noticed you were gone. I must have had seven people asked where you were. But what's worse is that Jeanette noticed Julia was missing."

James put his hands on his face, "Oh God. It's her dream to go study with Dr. Fallon."

"Yeah, that's what Ira told me."

"Shit!" James exclaimed, standing up and walking to the window. "Did I ruin her chance?"

Walter looked at him sympathetically as he packed James's pipe with tobacco, knowing he would want a smoke. "Ira arranged for Julia to eat lunch with Jeanette today. She seems to think Julia was feeling under the weather."

Walter brought the pipe to James and he began to smoke. James pondered all that Walter had told him when Walter added one more piece of advice. "James, you have to stay away from her today."

James turned from the window and back toward Walter. "I'm not sure that I can do that, nor do I want to."

Walter frowned, "James, listen to me. Think about Maude and the kids. Think about all you've stood for and believed. You have to leave this girl alone."

James rubbed his eyes before responding, "I have one more day and then will never see her again. For once, why can't I throw caution to the wind?"

"At least don't bother her until this evening. She has to show Jeanette that she's serious about studying with her and about her future. If she goes galavanting off with you again, that will not look good for her. Regardless of your own selfish wants, what is best for her is for you to back away for a few hours."

While listening, James finished his pipe and placed it in the ashtray. "I'll stay away during the day today," he said as he wobbled slowly toward the bathroom. However, James stopped dead in his tracks when he walked by the desk.

"Walter?" James called with trepidation.

"What is it James?"

"Have you touched anything on the desk?"

"Why do you ask?"

James slumped into the desk chair and laid his head on the desk.

Walter walked over and placed his hand on James's shoulder. "What's wrong?"

Silently, James picked up the letter. He handed it to Walter, never moving his head off the desk.

Walter quickly began to scan the letter. "You didn't."

James banged his already hurting head on the desk before responding, "I did. I wrote it a couple of nights ago after going to that party at William Taylor's mansion."

"And you think Julia saw it?"

"I know Julia saw it. It was on the shelf right there on top of the stationary."

Walter's bushy eyebrows raised in alarm. "Oh shit."

"Oh shit is right," James said morosely.

JAMES SIPPED HIS SODA as his hat hung low over his eyes, still trying to keep out the sun. Walter handed him the morning program and asked, "So what do you want to go hear, and don't tell me Roman antiquity, because I'm not stupid and I know what you would be doing."

Not looking up, James mumbled, "I don't want to see her right now anyway. I'm not sure how I face her after that letter."

"Well, let's forget about that for now. You need to go now, Ira is heading this way."

James quickly bounded out of the chair, grabbed an orange and headed the other way, deciding to go to a roundtable discussion on the working class during the American Revolution. He walked out of the back of the dining room and down the hall to the parlor where the roundtable would take place. He entered the room and saw a table full of water glasses on his left. James grabbed a glass and noticing the chairs in rows, took a seat in the right back corner, hoping to be inconspicuous. That failed quickly when Hugh Campbell sauntered in and sat next to James.

With a smirk, Hugh started, "So, Dr. Pashen, I have a question for you."

"Yes, Dr. Campbell?"

"Are you a fundamentalist or a liberal?"

Not expecting that question, James responded, "Why are you asking me this?"

"Well, it is the major question facing our church today. I figured a fine, learned man like yourself would have an opinion on the subject," Hugh stated.

James paused to consider Hugh's question before answering, "First off, the debate is not as strong in the Southern Presbyterian Church as it is in the Northern one, but I would most definitely fall with the liberals. I am a believer in the freedom of the conscience. What I believe and what you believe may be different, but we still worship the same God."

"But, James, surely you see that certain fundamentals must be believed in order to be Presbyterian?"

"I disagree, as long as I declare Christ as my Lord, then I am welcomed at the table and should be welcomed at the church."

Hugh was incredulous. "I bet you were one of those who enjoyed Fosdick's sermon, weren't you?"

"I will admit that Fosdick and I have very much the same outlook on the gospel and on faith," James said placidly hoping to calm Hugh down.

As other people began to file into the room, James and Hugh stopped their discussion of Presbyterian polity, but before Hugh moved to his own seat, he extended his hand and grasped James's. "Your speech the other day was excellent, but a word of advice, if you are ever looking to leave Virginia, don't let the other historians notice your actions with Miss O'Connor."

"We've been that obvious, haven't we?"

Hugh chuckled, "You could say that. Just remember this advice from one Presbyterian to another." Dr. Campbell patted James on the back before moving to sit with a colleague from Princeton.

TWO HOURS LATER, AFTER listening to a thorough discussion that fit nicely with his thesis, James walked down the hall back to the dining room to get another glass of water. The moment he walked out of the door, Ira, who was a much larger man than James, grabbed his elbow and frog-marched him down to the first open door and all but pushed James inside.

James panicked and knowing that if Ira hit him it would hurt something awful, quickly backed away from the angry large man. "Dr. Pashen, you should be ashamed of yourself!"

"Ira, just let me explain," James said still backpedaling.

"It's Dr. Grossman to you! I don't give you permission to refer to me like we are friends."

James hands shot into the air "Dr. Grossman, please, can we talk calmly?" James asked slowly moving around the small room, just out of Ira's reach.

Ira stopped stalking and found a seat in a comfortable leather chair. He gestured for James to sit across from him. James sat down, intentionally staying out of arm's reach. Ira glared at James while James looked down at the floral arrangement on the coffee table between them.

Ira started, "So do you have some explanation of why you are taking advantage of my star student?"

"Whoa!" James blurted. "Julia is certainly no pushover. She's incredibly bright and everything we have done together has been completely consensual."

Ira turned red as he responded, "So she did stay the night!"

James put his hands up again and stated, "I don't think so, but I honestly don't know for sure. I woke up still in my suit from last night, so I'm pretty sure nothing happened."

Ira exhaled a breath he didn't even realize he was holding. "You know you two's escapade almost ruined her future."

"Walter mentioned something like that. I'm so glad you were able to smooth that over with Dr. Fallon," James said sincerely.

"Well, I'm just glad she wasn't with us last night. She ate dinner with Walter and I but decided to go upstairs rather than join us for a night cap. So she didn't see Julia helping you to the elevator. I wouldn't have been able to explain that away. Plus, Dr. Fallon knows she is engaged, and what does that say about her character to her future mentor?"

James breathed in the scent of verbena flowers from the arrangement on the coffee table. After rubbing his face with his hands, James looked at Ira and mentioned, "Well if it helps anything, I'm not sure she wants to see me again anyway."

Ira shook his head. "Son, you must know nothing about women. The woman I saw last night would lasso the moon for you if you asked her."

"But what about Albert?"

"Oh she loves Albert too, but Albert is not here; you are."

James leaned back, ruminating on what Ira just said when Ira broke in once again. "I know this is the last day, but it's a big day for her. Let her be. Disappear. Do whatever you need to, but stay away from her today. She has to make a good impression on Jeanette. I will make your excuses if she is looking for you. But just go away. Please."

"Ira, I have only one more day to see her, and then she's gone and probably forever."

For the first time in the conversation, Ira looked sympathetic to James's plight. "I know, James, but if you actually really love her, and you're not just infatuated with her, you will do what is best for her."

James leaned forward onto his elbows and looked at Ira. "You're right, Dr. Grossman. I hate to admit it, but you're right."

"James, I've always liked you, but Julia is like a daughter to me. When I thought it was a harmless flirtation, I thought it would be fun to watch you follow her around all week. I've seen many boys and men try to turn Julia's head and they've always failed, but there is something between you two. This is going to be the most important day of her future career. You have to stay away from her today."

James nodded but said nothing for a moment. Instead he took out his pipe and tobacco and simply sat looking at the floral arrangement. Ira decided to take out a cigar and the two men smoked in silence as they came to an understanding. As smoke began to fill the room, James looked at Ira and said, "I guess it is my time to exit stage left."

James stood and extended his hand.

Ira shook it.

JAMES TRUDGED THROUGH the lobby with his head down and hat on, hoping not to be seen, especially by Julia. He had almost made it to the door when Walter's voice rang through the lobby.

"James! James!"

Rolling his eyes and grunting audibly, James stopped but did not turn around.

"Where are you going? You need to stay for the afternoon sessions." Walter said while walking around to face James.

"I'm going out."

"Why?"

James thought about what he could say before telling Walter the truth. "Ira and I talked and we think it would be best for Julia if I disappeared for the rest of the day."

Walter looked at James, as if examining him for a brain injury. "Are you crazy? When I told you to stay away from her, I just meant until after her luncheon. And as much as I love Maude, I know what you feel about Julia doesn't happen very often. You have only one more day and you're going to leave her without saying goodbye?"

James's lip quivered before answering, "Walter, I have to do what's best for her, for herself, and for her future."

"James, you have to reconsider. What if you never see her again?"

"Then I will treasure these few days for the rest of my life."

Walter shook his head in pity. "I understand. Where will you go?"

James pondered this question for a bit then replied, "I'm not sure, Walter, but I'll be back in time to catch the train tomorrow."

James turned and walked out of the hotel and into the salt-filled air.

Julia frowned from the other side of the lobby.

Chapter 19
The Maze

JAMES DUCKED HIS HEAD and stepped into the cab. "Vizcaya, please."

"Mr. James! It's you!"

"Samuel!" James said, smiling for the first time all day.

"So you just can't stay away from the lure of the great mansion, huh. I knew you would love it!"

"Samuel, you've been a true friend this week. I'm glad you have been my driver here," James noted before leaning back into the seat. Samuel pulled out of the hotel drive and headed toward the causeway to the mainland. James bowed his head and silently prayed for forgiveness for his choices this week before looking out toward the towering sun.

After a few minutes of driving, Samuel asked, "So where is the beautiful girl?"

"She is back at the hotel where she belongs."

Samuel frowned sympathetically. "She's a sweet woman. But it's better that you leave her alone. Nothing good can come of seeing her."

James laughed sarcastically, "Trust me, Samuel, I've heard that speech enough today."

"Nothing good can come from falling in love in Miami, Mr. James."

James looked into the rearview mirror into Samuel's eyes. "Unfortunately, it is too late for that advice."

"Oh, Mr. James, you should have listened to me on the first day. I told you what Miami would do to you."

"I know."

James turned his head away and became quiet.

Focusing on the Floridian flora that sped past the car, James did not notice as the cab sped through the gates to Vizcaya.

JAMES TOOK THE STEPS one at a time, looking over the facade of the house. Not sure what he would do or say, James knocked on the gated door and waited patiently for someone to answer. After a few moments, a small gray-haired butler dressed in coat tails answered the door, asking, "May I help you?"

James, looking down at him slightly, replied, "Is Mr. Taylor available?"

"Let me see if he is up to taking..."

"Dr. Pashen! So good to see you again!" Mr. Taylor cut it as he rounded the corner and saw James in the door.

"Mr. Taylor," James stated. "I apologize for imposing on you without an invitation."

"Nonsense! I'm glad you're here. Would you join me for a drink and tell me what brought you here today?" Mr. Taylor motioned toward the courtyard for James to join him there.

James followed Mr. Taylor, who was dressed in casual slacks and an white button-down shirt. After a moment, James said, "Well, I just needed to get away from the conference, and out of all the places in Miami, this is the one I wanted to spend more time at. I hope you are ok with that."

The men sat across from each other and Mr. Taylor instructed the butler to bring two scotches. James stepped in and asked for a soda, adding, "I had a little too much to drink last night, so I'm going to take it easy today."

Mr. Taylor asked, "Can I at least interest you in a cigar? It's the finest money can buy."

"How can I pass that up?"

Mr. Taylor opened his wooden cigar box and took two Cuban cigars out. Taylor reached over and handed James the cigar and proceeded to light it. They sat back and enjoyed the rich cigar before Mr. Taylor asked James, "What ever happened with the woman from the other night?"

"What hasn't happened with the woman!"

The butler brought each man his drink and they sat in a comfortable silence, enjoying the breezy afternoon in the courtyard. Eventually Mr. Taylor asked, "So what did you do to screw it up?"

James looked up from his Coca-Cola but didn't say anything. Taylor continued, "Come on! You show up on my doorstep unannounced in the middle of the day. Either you screwed up or she's gone. I'm betting on screwed up. So you just left the conference today rather than talk to her. Am I right?"

"I had to. Her future depended on her talking to this Dr. Fallon today, and I would be in the way. Furthermore, there is no future; there is only heartache and guilt ahead."

Mr. Taylor shook his head in disappointment before continuing, "Do you remember what we talked about the night you came to the party?"

James took a deep breath before taking a sip of his Coca-Cola. "I do."

"Then seize the moment, son!"

"But why? There's nothing to do about it. There's no future."

"You're right. There's not a future, but that doesn't mean you shouldn't grasp on to the little bit of love you can receive from her. Live in the present. In the now. Like the Bible verse says, 'Be not therefore anxious for the morrow: for the morrow will be anxious for itself.'"

James chuckled and shook his head. "I'm pretty sure Jesus isn't talking about me having an affair with Miss O'Connor."

Mr. Taylor joined in laughter, "Probably not, but you get my point. For today, don't worry about tomorrow. Worry about today. Worry about her."

"I do see the wisdom in your point of view, but if I truly love her, I have to do what is best for her first," James said contemplatively.

"But don't you think she should decide what is best for her," Mr. Taylor argued. "It sounds to me as if everyone, including yourself, is deciding what is best for her. Ask her what she thinks. Include her in your decisions."

James took a deep drag on the cigar while looking at Mr. Taylor. He looked up to the open sky above the courtyard and said, "Would you mind if I wandered the gardens for a little while?"

"Be my guest! I am quite proud of them."

"Thank you Mr. Taylor for the cigar and for listening. You've given me a lot to ponder."

They stood and shook hands.

Mr. Taylor patted him on the arm. "If you need anything else, feel free to come back to the house."

James thanked him and began to walk out the back door to head out to the garden.

Once James was around the corner, Mr. Taylor called to the butler. "I need you to make a phone call for me."

HIS HEART HEAVY, JAMES wandered aimlessly around the garden for quite a while enjoying the beautiful greens and lush flowers. Enveloped by the smell of salt water and flora, James was in a walking daze before deciding to head to the maze where he had found Julia a couple of nights before. As he entered, he bowed his head and began to pray quietly, "Lord, I have always believed in providence, that you have a plan and a reason for things. I've trusted that and have lived by that my entire life. So, I'm lost. I just don't understand. I don't believe you would have put her into my life for no reason, but I don't see the reason. I knew when Maude came into my life. I knew when I met Walter what his place was going to be, but I have no clue why Julia was introduced into my life and what this means."

Walking slowly through the labyrinth, James continued his prayer in desperation, "You wouldn't put me through this if there wasn't a reason, God. So what is it? Why did I meet Julia?"

Out of words, James continued blankly walking, hoping to hear something, anything from God. The silence became deafening before James exclaimed, "I know you're there, God! I know you hear me! And I know you have a plan for my future. But I don't see it! For the first time in my life, I am lost. I am lost without a compass, God. Where is my North Star?"

"Well, considering that you are pointing South, and it's still daylight, you might have some issues finding it."

James spun around, startled by her voice. Trying to catch his breath, James looked incredulously at her. "What are you doing here?"

Julia smiled wryly at him, "I got a message at the hotel that you were here. So I got a taxi and came over."

She sat down on a bench situated on the outside of the maze and patted the bench, beckoning him to sit with her. Slowly, James made his way out of the maze and sat down.

"So tell me about it," Julia commanded.

"Where should I start?"

"Let's start with this prayer. What are you praying about?"

James put his hands on his knees and looked forward. "Well, when you walked up I was praying about how, for the first time in my life, I have no direction. No purpose. No goal."

"And before?"

"About why you - what is the reason you are in my life now."

"And what did you figure out?" Julia asked.

"Nothing. Nothing at all."

"Did you ever think it was not God but the devil that brought us together?"

James quietly considered this possibility for a minute, before responding, "I guess that could be possible."

James rubbed his eyes and sat up straight. Julia touched his arm lightly which sent a jolt of the recognition of home through him.

"Your letter was beautiful."

James turned toward her but looked over her head and out toward the main garden. "I didn't mean for you to see that."

"I know, but I'm glad I did." Julia wrapped her hand around his elbow. "I don't know how I feel about how strongly you feel about me. How can you know already that you love me?"

James's eyes focused on hers. "When I realized that night, after dancing with you, that I may never be able to have you close to me again, that sense of loss was so sudden and deep and I felt so empty that I knew something important had just happened. I've only felt that a few times in my life and every time it was after I lost someone I loved."

James took her hand in his and continued, "So that's how I know I love you. I was never going to voice it, but you already know."

They sat in companionable silence for a while, listening to the light crash of the ocean waves and the birds chirping in the trees. James reached his left hand and covered her left hand that was still attached to his elbow.

Eventually Julia asked, "So what do we do?"

"I have no idea. It all ends tomorrow regardless."

"True, but we still have tonight."

James squeezed her hand tight, hoping to avoid the subject at hand. "How did your lunch go with Dr. Fallon? Did you get that all settled?"

"Yes, she was very gracious, and it looks like I will be studying under her in the fall."

"I'm so happy to hear that," he said as he took her hand from his elbow and kissed it.

"But I don't want to talk about the future."

"Then what do you want to talk about?" James asked.

"Tonight."

"What do you want to do?"

Julia raised her hand to his cheek and kissed him. Then she leaned into his right ear and whispered, "Something we will remember and cherish forever."

Chapter 20
The Night

JAMES AND JULIA WALKED hand in hand out of the garden, both blushing slightly at the implications of their conversation earlier. As they walked towards the front of the house, Mr. Taylor came out to greet them.

"Miss O'Connor! Dr. Pashen! I wasn't sure I'd get to see you again before you left."

Julia greeted him joyfully, "Thank you for the message, Mr. Taylor!"

She ribbed James as she continued, "I'm glad someone let me make my own decision."

Mr. Taylor beamed at her joke, "It was nothing. I'm glad you got the message in time."

Julia walked to Mr. Taylor and placed a kiss on his cheek. "Thank you again for everything. Vizcaya will always have a place in my heart."

James extended his hand to shake Mr. Taylor's when Taylor asked, "May I offer my car to drive you back to the Flamingo?"

The couple acquiesced to the suggestion and soon they were climbing into the light brown Biddle Sedan's back seat as Mr. Taylor's driver sat in front of the them. James took Julia's hand and pulled her close to him as the car jetted out of the driveway and onto the main road.

She placed her hand on his leg as he leaned in and quietly asked, "Are you sure you want to do this?"

She turned and kissed him, her hand moving to his neck. She stared at him with desire, "Don't forget I suggested this. The real question is do you want to?"

James pulled away slightly and placed his forehead on hers. "I want to, yes. But I've never made this choice before."

"Neither have I, but I know this is right," Julia said. "Isn't that the words you used?"

"Yes it is."

She pulled him in and kissed him again.

"This is right."

IT WAS AFTER SUNDOWN by the time the car got them back to the hotel. While they were in the cab, they discussed the need to split up when they got to the hotel. James would go find them some wine and snacks while Julia would go to her room and freshen up. They agreed to meet in James's room at 8:00.

After procuring a bottle of Bordeaux and some cheese and crackers from a waiter who was happy with his tip, James used the stairs to walk up to his room. James opened the door to 316 and laid the wine and food on the desk next to the letter. James peeked at the clock and realized he had 45 minutes until Julia would arrive, he decided to shower and shave before Julia came to the room.

Time seemed to speed by and before he knew it, the clock read eight. Shortly after, he heard her soft knock. Dressed in a white buttoned-down shirt and blue pants, James opened the door to let Julia in.

She sashayed in with black hose up to her knees. Her black skirt just above her knee, it was obvious to James that she had spent some time getting ready as well.

James closed the door as she twirled around and smiled at him, "Do you like what you see?"

James just stared at her admiring her beauty when she jabbed, "That was not a rhetorical question."

James smiled broadly, "Well, you definitely have IT."

She bounced over to him and kissed him before asking, "So what did you find us to eat? I'm starving."

"I was able to find us some cheese and crackers. I also procured for us a bottle of wine."

"May I have a glass?"

James left the doorway and walked to the desk and poured two glasses of wine. Handing her one, he began to sip on the Bordeaux as he sat down in the chair at the desk. He immediately felt the blur of warmth flooding his veins. Julia came to the desk and grabbed some of the crackers and began to eat.

They both quickly ate several crackers and cheese before turning back to the wine. Julia walked over to the window and looked out into the night. James followed her and wrapped his arms around her stomach and began to kiss her neck.

She tilted her head for a moment, reveling in the feeling of intimacy before she turned her head and smiled. She kissed him once before looking back outside the window. "You have a much better view in your room than I do in mine."

Still holding on to her, he looked down and told her the story of watching the tennis match his first day in the room. She then asked, "Is that the pool down there?" pointing to some sliver of moonlight reflecting off of the water.

"Yes, it was usually busy during the times I was in here during the day."

"Let's go down there!"

He looked incredulous. "Right now?"

"Of course, I love night swimming!" She looked at him beaming.

"Doesn't the pool close at sundown?"

"We leave tomorrow. What are they going to do, kick us out of the hotel?"

FIFTEEN MINUTES LATER, Julia was removing her clothing, leaving on her silk chemise before stepping to the edge of the pool. "Come on James, no one is coming. Get in the water with me."

Looking around one more time, James began to unbutton his shirt slowly. Julia jumped into the water then swam to the wall and propped her head on her arms and watched him avidly. Eventually James was left in nothing but his boxers. Julia raised her eyebrow flirtatiously before telling him, "I promise the water is more comfortable than the cold air!" James made sure the string on the boxers was tied tight then dove in and swam to where she was.

"This was an excellent idea," he said as his head popped out of the water a few feet from her.

"I told you how much I loved the water. I prefer the ocean but a pool will do just fine for us tonight."

James floated on his back for a moment before leisurely swimming the backstroke around the pool. He swam away and back towards her a few times before stopping. "The water feels amazing," James said.

Julia smiled and dove her head under the water before popping back up in front of James. He pulled her close and kissed her once before she sunk back into the water like a mermaid heading home. When her head popped above the water again, James asked, "So when is your train tomorrow?"

"No discussion of tomorrow," Julia ordered. "We only worry about tonight."

She ducked back under the water and swam to one of the walls. She propped herself up by her arms, looking out over the palm trees. James swam beside her and mimicked her pose.

"It's just so peaceful and beautiful. I never want to forget this moment," Julia declared.

James turned his head to her and saw a few stray hairs that had gotten loose in the water. He delicately used his right hand to move them back behind her ear. His hand moved and began to play with her hair as she turned and looked into his eyes. She leaned into him and began to kiss him.

Julia's hands moved to James's neck as they turned fully facing each other. Their bodies flush together as their hands began to explore each other. James grabbed her tight and swam them both to a part of the pool where they could stand. She locked her legs around him as he caressed her hip.

He lightly began kissing her neck as the water danced around them. Julia's arms wrapped tight around his neck and her head was thrown back to give him access to her neck. She let out a soft moan as he nibbled at her neck, his hands moving to her sides and beginning to grope for the edges of her chemise.

As James found the material and began to lift it up, Julia raised her arms so he could pull it off her. As soon as it was off, he threw it and she was instantly kissing his neck. Her legs released his body as her hands fumbled around his boxers to find the string. Pulling it untied as his hands played with her hair, she pulled the boxers off of him before placing her legs around him once again. James put his hands on her hips and lifted her up slightly. Pulling him tight to her and kissing him, Julia mumbled into his mouth, "Yes."

JAMES'S ARM WAS AROUND Julia as they laid in the bed in room 316. As he kissed the top of her head, she smiled and said, "I thought you'd be asleep by now."

"And miss the last few hours of our life together? I'd rather be tired tomorrow."

"We have to sleep at some point! We can't do this all night long!"

James laughed as he lightly played with her upper arm, "Are you sure about that? Don't you want to find out?"

Julia mumbled under her breath and rolled her eyes, "Men."

"What was that?" James joked loudly.

She turned and propped her arm across his chest. "So tell me what would your life be like?"

"What do you mean?"

Julia gazed at him. "Let's say there was no Albert and no Maude. What would our lives be like?"

James put his hands behind his head and thought out loud, "Well, let's see here. With where I am in my career, I'm at a place where I could begin to move on. I'd probably try to find something in New York while you went to graduate school and studied under Dr. Fallon. Then I'd follow you wherever you would want your career to lead. If we decided to have children, maybe I'd just be a house husband and write odes to the long dead South."

Running her fingers along his chest, she responded, "Would you have become Catholic for me?"

"Would I have to be rebaptized?"

"No, we don't require Protestants to be rebaptized as long as they were baptized in the name of the Father, Son, and Holy Ghost."

"And what would our home life be like?" James asked thoughtfully.

"Full of debates and discussions, but also full of joy," Julia smiled, kissing his chest.

"It's a fun dream to think about."

"Yes it is."

Julia continued to lazily draw on his chest before looking up and asking, "Are you sleepy?"

"No, not really. What did you have in mind?"

Julia smiled and began to kiss down his chest.

Day 6
Thursday, January 10, 1924

Chapter 21
The Proposition

AS THE EARLY MORNING sunlight danced through the window, James gently played with Julia's hair that was splayed out across his chest. James let her sleep as he laid there thinking about the last week. He twirled her brown hair in his fingers pondering if there was any way he could slow down time and stop the end from coming.

He took a mental picture of the woman laying on his chest, knowing this would be the last morning he'd ever see her. He closed his eyes to cherish the moment when in his mind, he saw another possibility. He and Julia holding hands as they walked to the railing of a passenger ship... laying together in a cramped railroad car... standing in the French countryside... fixing dinner in a cramped Roman apartment... debating each other's research over glasses of wine... what an incredible life that would be, he thought to himself.

Julia's eyes fluttered open and she noticed the content smile on James's face.

"Good morning," she whispered loudly.

James opened his eyes and smiled, "Good morning, Sunshine."

"What were you smiling about?"

"Just thinking about you is all."

"Is all, huh?" She joked with him.

"Maybe I should have said - Only you," he ribbed as he leaned down and kissed her forehead.

Julia crawled up his body and kissed him.

James drew her closer to him and asked her, "How much more time do we have?"

Julia turned and looked at the clock, "Maybe two hours until I'll need to go pack."

James began to move his hands lower on her as he said, "Then we have plenty of time."

"SO I HAVE A PROPOSITION for you."

"A proposition?"

"Yes. A proposition."

"And what would that be?"

"Run away with me." James said succinctly.

Julia propped up but didn't say anything.

James turned red and began to fidget.

"Well?" James asked after a long period of silence.

"You can't be serious. Surely you're just feeding me a line."

"I'm completely on the level."

Julia looked at him with a scared look on her face. "Have you even thought this through? Where would we go? What would we do? How would we survive?"

"I have a plan."

"And how long have you been thinking about this said 'plan?'"

James shrugged, "Maybe two hours?"

Julia incredulously said, "And you are asking me to throw my entire life and future away and go God knows where with you? Are you screwy?"

James took a deep breath to settle himself. "I have it all mapped out."

"And pray tell me what this wonderful, glorious, well-thought out plan is?"

James sat up and began, "Instead of boarding trains bound for home today, we would go to the docks and take a ship to Havana. Once in Havana, we could decide what part of Europe we would go to and catch a passenger ship across the ocean. Because of my past research, I have a few contacts in England and Scotland who could help us with finding employment or finding a school for you."

Julia rolled her eyes but kept asking questions. "And where will the money for all this come from?"

"I have quite a bit with me, enough to get us across the ocean and settled in Europe." James looked at her earnestly, and continued, "I love you. You know that. We would be very happy together."

Julia got out of bed and began to put on her clothes, "And what about Maude and your children? You would just abandon them and leave them penniless?"

"I have a plan for that too. I have a good life insurance policy, I was going to ask Samuel to help us fake our deaths and get new identities. Then we would leave Miami and never come back."

Dressed in her clothes from last night, Julia began to pace the room while James sat under the covers on the bed. She kept looking at him and then turning away. Finally, she looked at him and said, "I can't."

James hung his head, expecting this answer. He could already feel the hole forming in his heart, but he knew she was right.

Julia continued, "James, I love you, but."

"Stop there," James said. "Leave it there. I don't want to hear the but."

Julia sat down on the edge of the bed, looking away from where he was sitting. "If I could split myself in two, and give you one and give Albert one, I would. But I can't. As wonderful as this week has been and as incredible as last night was, this was the deal we made. This is how it has to be. As dear as you are to me, your children need you more. Your wife needs you more. I will cherish this week forever, but this is all it can ever be."

James tried to hold back tears as he listened, knowing she was right. His children did need their father. His wife needed her husband. And he knew, although unsaid, that she needed Albert. He knew she was right.

She turned to look at him one last time. She leaned in and kissed him once.

James looked at her, despondent. "I love you."

"I love you, too."

Julia grabbed her bag and James laid down and turned away from her. She walked by the desk then out of the door.

Chapter 22
The Driver Revisited

JAMES COULD NOT BRING himself to get out of bed. He knew that he was supposed to check out in 30 minutes, but he just didn't give a damn. Laying on his stomach, all he wanted to do was waste away until the pain in his chest was gone. It felt as if a part of him had been ripped out and would never return again.

Nevertheless, he got himself out of bed and put on a plain white dress shirt and brown slacks. Forgoing a shower, James began to throw things into his suitcase. Moving around the room in a daze, he figured he was leaving something, but he knew he just needed to get out of this room, out of Miami, out of this existence he had chosen for himself.

He picked up the suitcase and looked back at the bed one more time. The greatest night of his life happened there, but so did the worst morning. Turning around, he did not look back as he left room 316 forever.

JAMES PLODDED ALONG the lobby to the front desk. His suitcase in hand and his hat hiding his eyes, he paid his bill for the week before walking silently out of the lobby and to the nearest cab.

Never looking up, he muttered to the driver, "To the railway station."

The driver looked into the rear-view mirror and smiled brightly, "Mr. James! I get to see you one more time before you leave!"

Still looking down, James babbled, "Hello Samuel."

"I know that look, Mr. James," Samuel noted solemnly. "That is the look of heartbreak that Miami brings to people."

James looked out at the water of the bay as they sped slowly across the causeway, thinking that if she had said yes, their lives would be so different. They would be faking their deaths today and about to board a boat to Havana.

Instead he was alone in the back of the yellow cab, heading back to Charlottesville, to Maude, to real life.

"I am so sorry the heat of Miami got you," Samuel said. "You have been a joy to get to drive around these last few days."

James nodded appreciatively as the yellow cab rolled into downtown Miami and toward the train station. Outside the cab, the boom town was bustling with construction and automobiles. Inside the cab, James's life seemed to be busted. Stuck in his thoughts and his hollow feeling, James stared down at his feet wondering if he would ever feel right again.

"Mr. James, is there anything I can do for you?"

James said nothing at first, pondering Samuel's offer. Finally, James looked up and said, "Have you ever heard of the nursery rhyme, Humpty Dumpty?"

"Why do you ask?"

"Because I'm not sure that all the king's horses or all the king's men can put me back together again."

"Mr. James, please heed my advice this time," Samuel implored.

"I might as well start listening now," James responded. "What is your advice?"

" Two things. First, the sooner you accept the guilt from the choices you made, the better you can live the rest of your life. Second, never speak of this week again. Not with your friend. Not with the girl. Not with the owner of the mansion. No one. If it must stay alive, let it stay in your head, but never speak of it."

James rolled his eyes, but said nothing.

Samuel noticed and his memory came rushing back.

Miami, Florida - October 15, 1915 - "Helen, please don't do this!"

"Samuel, I just can't live like this anymore!"

"I'll work harder. I'll pick up more shifts. Soon I could own my own taxi and all the profit will be ours."

Helen, dressed in a much finer dress than a taxi driver could ever afford, took a slow drag off her cigarette and said, "I don't know why I even ever fell for you. My daddy warned me about poor white trash but I just saw you and thought love could overcome poverty. But you're just like all the rest of those poor boys. Sure you work hard and treat me nice, but we can't afford any of the things I like, and I'm tired of it."

Helen's blond hair swung a bit as she picked up her suitcase as Samuel pleaded, "You don't want to do this! We were happy here in Miami. Please don't go!" He jumped up from the small wooden table and walked around it toward her.

"I love you, Helen! We can be happy. Money isn't everything!" He begged as he took her hand.

Helen looked at him pitifully and responded. "I used to think like you do."

"What changed?" He asked desperately.

She grimaced a little but answered him, "I realized that love is not as important as money."

Helen removed her hands from his, and after picking up her suitcase, walked out of the door. Samuel went to the window and watched her as she was picked up by a man in an expensive suit. She climbed into the car. Helen leaned in and kissed the man once before the car they were in sped off.

Samuel begged James, "You must move on and forget this place! You must go back home and pretend as if none of this happened. Please believe me! Please do this!"

James looked up from his crouched position and looked out of the front of the windshield, "I will listen to you this time."

SITTING ON A BENCH on the platform of the train station, James took a swig of his flask before bowing his head down. James tapped his feet as his hat continued to cover his eyes. He hoped no one would notice him. He wasn't up to talking to anyone, so instead he took out a copy of *The Able McLaughlins* and began to read.

Slowly, the platform filled up with other people heading north as well. James, on the far end of the platform, silently prayed that none of his friends would find him. Hold the book in such a way to cover his face, James lost track of the movement of people around him until he heard the train whistle followed by grinding of steel wheels on the track. He peered over his book to find the platform nearly full. Scanning the crowd, the only people he knew nearby were Walter and Jeanette, hand-in-hand. Deciding he had no interest in seeing either of them, James pulled his hat down low again and began to gather his things to board the train.

James walked to the car in which he had a single compartment reserved for himself and showed his ticket to the porter who pointed him to his room. Quickly and quietly, James moved down the thin hall and entered his compartment, shutting the door behind him. Putting his things down, he sat on the bench and grabbed his book. Determined not to look outside, he began to drown his sorrows in the written word.

But the words began to swirl on the page and he thought to himself, *Who have I become?* He began to realize that the hole in his heart was not just for the lose of Julia, but for the lose of the man he had been. Loyal, honorable, faithful. Those things were gone, and in its place, a hole which he had to hide from everyone at home, because no one could find out about who he really was. No one could know he had committed adultery. No one could know he had betrayed Maude, betrayed his family, betrayed himself.

After about fifteen minutes, James looked at his watch and realized the train would not leave for another ten minutes. He put his book down and stared blankly out the window of the compartment. After a few minutes of staring at nothing, he looked down.

Dressed in a black cloche hat and a short black dress stood Julia, less than three feet away on the other side of the window. James, once again, could not take his eyes off of her.

The hole in his chest felt empty again as he watched her standing in line to board the train. Her eyes were puffy as if she had been crying, but she held her head up high. James needed to look away but couldn't. Eventually she turned and looked into the window and saw him.

Their eyes locked, both understanding what the look really meant.

She nodded her head once before the line moved and she walked out of sight.

Epilogue
The Photograph

HER PHONE VIBRATED on the table as she read what seemed to be the eight-hundredth letter from a university asking William Taylor for money. Obviously not much had changed in the past 90 years in terms of how universities built their endowments, she mused. Ignoring her phone, she began to type notes into her MacBook about the size of the donation the University of Chicago was asking for and the date. She planned to search for a corresponding letter from Taylor when she flew back to Chicago tomorrow.

With only three months to go until her thesis was due for submission to her readers, tracking down the last parts of her research had become a burden on her life. Her phone vibrated again, and huffing she picked up the phone. She had one message. "I can't wait to see you tomorrow!" She rolled her eyes at Kevin's text, frustrated because he knew she only had a few hours left of research time. Deciding she would deal with him later, she placed the phone back down and went back to reading correspondence.

She placed her cardigan over her shoulders when the air conditioner kicked on. Brushing her pink-streaked hair out of her face, the woman examined the letter in front of her and chuckled. Evidently her advisor's job was originally paid for because of the letter the University of Chicago sent that she was holding in her hand. Grabbing her phone, she took a quick picture of the letter and sent it to her advisor, noting, "I should have known that you were waiting for me to find this letter before you'd let me finish researching." Putting the phone back down, she took a few more notes as an older lady limped toward her.

"Miss Williams, the archives here at Vizcaya will close for the day in one hour. Is there anything in particular you would like to examine before we close?" the older lady asked nicely.

"Can you give me a few minutes to read back over my notes, to see what I might be missing?" Miss Williams asked politely.

"Sure, sugar. I'll be right back."

The older lady turned and hobbled back to her desk as Miss Williams scrolled up on her Word document. She began reading through all her notes from both Tuesday and today. Silently cursing that she needed more time at the archives before flying back to Chicago, she decided that perhaps looking through photographs she might gain a bit more insight into William Taylor's philanthropism, which was the major focus of her doctoral thesis.

Motioning to the archivist behind the desk, Miss Williams picked up her phone and texted Kevin, "My flight leaves Miami around six in the morning so I should be at O'Hare by nine."

The archivist's limp took her a moment before getting to the table and asking, "Did you decide?"

"Could I look at your photo collection? Specifically, I am looking for photos with Mr. Taylor in them."

"Of course, Miss Williams, I'll be right back with that collection."

Her phone buzzed again as the archivist moved slowly toward the resource room. Miss Williams read Kevin's response but did not see a reply from her advisor. She placed the phone back down and pulled her MacBook to her. She typed into Google, "William Taylor University of Chicago." As the results popped up, several pictures of her advisor and his family populated the top of the page. Scrolling past those, she eventually found an article on page three she had not read before. She began to take notes on the article from the Chicago Tribune when the archivist slowly made her way back to the table with the photographs.

"Here you go, Miss Williams," handing the box of photographs over to her. "If you need anything else, please feel free to ask me," the archivist said smiling before shuffling towards her desk.

Miss Williams immediately began thumbing through the photographs, picking them up one at a time and examining them. After looking at a few pictures, she flipped one over with her right hand that was adorned with rings. She realized that the date and people were written on the back. Going back through the first few, not all of them had writing on them, but Miss Williams decided to notate the ones that did.

She began to notice a pattern. Taylor had known probably every famous person in the early 1920s. There were pictures of Taylor with Presidents, captains of industry, movie stars, and many more. What was even more fascinating is these pictures would often have random academics standing next to these famous people.

Miss Williams grabbed her phone to check the time. Realizing she only had about thirty more minutes, she began to spread the pictures out across the tables in the archives room. Walking around the tables, she glanced at each one, not really paying any attention to details. She grabbed her iPhone and began taking snaps of the photographs to be able to examine them later.

Going from table to table, she tapped the red circle on her phone then flipping the pictures over, she took a picture again. Over and over she did this as fast as she could, just finishing with the last table of pictures. The archivist, now using a cane, clomped over to tell Miss Williams that it was time to clean up and get ready to leave.

"So I hope you have enjoyed your visit to Miami!" the archivist beamed.

"I have! Being here at Vizcaya has been a particular delight."

"Will we see you again, Miss Williams?" the archivist asked as Miss Williams packed up.

"Hopefully not! I feel like I've been researching Mr. Taylor for far too long. But if I need more, I will definitely be back!"

"Well safe travels home, sugar."

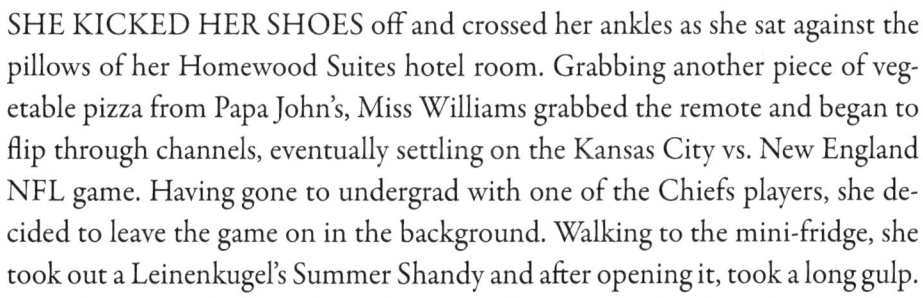

SHE KICKED HER SHOES off and crossed her ankles as she sat against the pillows of her Homewood Suites hotel room. Grabbing another piece of vegetable pizza from Papa John's, Miss Williams grabbed the remote and began to flip through channels, eventually settling on the Kansas City vs. New England NFL game. Having gone to undergrad with one of the Chiefs players, she decided to leave the game on in the background. Walking to the mini-fridge, she took out a Leinenkugel's Summer Shandy and after opening it, took a long gulp.

After sitting back on the bed, Miss Williams picked up her phone and began to scan through the pictures she had taken that afternoon. She took notes on each picture, examining the writings on the back of them. Swiping right, she would read the descriptions before looking at the picture. After about 30 photos, she came to one that had no description. Swiping right, she began to examine it closely. She immediately saw Taylor and a famous movie star from the 20s, before trying to figure out the other two people in the picture.

She stammered out loud, "Holy Shit!"

Staring at the picture again, she zoomed it in some. She was sure she knew who the man standing next to Taylor is. Going to the messages app on her iPhone, she scrolled down until she found her conversation with Dad. She tapped on it and typed, "Do you have a minute?"

He immediately responded, "Sure Lauren, what's up?"

She texted back, "I'm going to send you a photo. Hold on."

Lauren selected the photo she had been staring at and pushed the blue arrow to send it to her father.

Almost as soon as the photo went through, her ringtone from "The Last of the Mohicans" began to erupt from her iPhone.

"Hey, Dad!"

Not even saying hello, he immediately asked, "Where did you find this?"

"In Miami."

"I had forgotten about your trip to do research."

"Do you think that's really him?" Lauren asked carefully.

"It sure looks like him, but none of the family stories I've heard ever mention him traveling to Miami," her dad responded.

"Do you have any pictures nearby?" Lauren asked, beginning to pace the room.

"No I don't," he said. "They are all kept at the family farm down near Eufaula."

Lauren stopped at the desk and grabbed her MacBook.

"Dad, I have a couple of pictures uploaded on ancestry.com. Let me log on. Hold on."

She went silent as she typed in her login information and began to look at her family tree.

Finding the pictures, she spoke, "Looking at the pictures I have uploaded of him, and looking at his birth and death dates, he would be the right age for this picture. Furthermore, he fits the type of person Taylor would have met. Dad, I'm almost positive it's him."

"But then what is he doing at a party with one of the richest men in America and a movie star?" her dad asked. "And where was Maude if he was there? Because that's definitely not Maude in that picture with him. I remember Great-Grand Maude."

Both were silent for a moment, contemplating what they knew.

Lauren eventually spoke, "Unfortunately, there is no note on that picture. I don't think I can even pinpoint the year."

"All your research on Taylor this past year, and you've found no mention of him?"

Lauren thought carefully through all her work. "I don't think so, Dad. The last name of Pashen is a rather unique one. I think it would have jumped out at me if I had come across it in my research."

"Well, your granddad has a few pictures of him at the old farmhouse. I'll go down there tomorrow and see if I can find anything else that might help us figure out why he was in Miami and at Taylor's house."

"And maybe you'll find something about who this woman is."

LAUREN WALKED DOWN the corridor of the nearly abandoned Social Science Research Building, heading to the office of Dr. Brandon Higgins, her advisor. Frustrated that this meeting was on a Sunday, her footsteps sounded like stomps echoing down the empty hall towards the office of the William Deering Taylor Endowed Chair of American History.

She wondered if he would finally tell her she had enough research done. She had thought for many weeks that she had enough information to be able to tell the story of William Taylor and his philanthropy, but Higgins had continually pushed her to find more. Lauren would begrudgingly admit that her advisor had been right. The information she found on this trip to Miami would be invaluable to her argument.

After she knocked and he bade her to come in, she sat in the standard student chair across from the aluminum industrial desk found in his office. Laying her backpack down next to her chair, Lauren began taking out her MacBook to get ready to discuss the research.

"So how was Miami?" Higgins began politely, leaning back in his desk chair and looking at her with his hazel eyes.

"Hot and panicky," Lauren responded, looking up. "Everyone was getting ready for Irma to make landfall."

"Well, I'm glad you're here this morning instead of Miami."

"Me too," she replied. "However, I don't want to sound too spoiled, but why are we meeting now instead of tomorrow?"

"You know the book I'm researching on the 1968 Democratic National Convention," Higgins mentioned.

"Yes, did you get her?"

"I got her. I will interview her tomorrow night in Los Angeles."

Lauren smiled excitedly, "That's wonderful. I can't believe you convinced her."

"Well, it took months of negotiating, but I get an hour on the record and an hour off."

"Could you get my dad an autograph? He always had a crush on her."

Higgins chuckled, "I'll see what I can do. Ok, so show me where you are at now."

Lauren opened her MacBook and emailed the research to him, including the pictures that she had taken of the photographs in the archives at Vizcaya. As he began to read through her notes, she decided to stand up and walk over to his bookshelf. Having been taught by her parents to always examine people's books to figure out who they are, she often perused Higgins books, finding his choices endlessly fascinating. Going to a section of the shelves she had never looked through before, she noticed several older books that were hiding near a corner of a shelf.

Always fascinated by antique books, she picked up one off the shelf and began to flip through the pages on an old book about the settlement house movement. After a few minutes, she placed that one down and picked up another. Higgins, being used to Lauren's book obsession, kept perusing her research. After about fifteen minutes of silence, Lauren came across a book covered in dust. Knowing it had not been moved in years, she gently picked it up and saw the title *Poor White Trash* embossed on the cover.

She turned around and began to speak, "Why do you have a copy of my great-great grandfather's book?"

At the same time as Lauren spoke, Dr. Higgins had said, "Why do you have a picture of my great grandmother?"

They both responded, "What?"

Dr. Higgins said again, "Why do you have a picture of my great grandmother?"

Laura, holding the book limply in her hand, stared dumbfounded at her advisor.

"Well?" he asked, breaking her from her trance.

She stammered for a moment before answering, "Which picture is it?"

He turned his laptop toward her and staring back at her was the picture she had been obsessed with for days.

Lauren examined the photo for a moment. "That's your great grandmother?!?" she asked amazed.

"I'm positive. In fact, let me show you something."

Dr. Higgins stook up and grabbed an old photo album from the shelf behind his desk. He placed the album on his desk and turned to the third page. "Do you see that picture right there?" Higgins pointed to the one at the top left. "That is my great grandmother Julia on her wedding day in 1924."

Lauren scooted her chair closer to the desk and stared at the photo. "Good God, her hairstyle is exactly the same, too! I wonder if these pictures were taken within the same year."

Higgins quickly opened his desk drawer and took out a magnifying glass. "I wish we had the original picture here but this will have to do for right now." He began to look at the picture on the computer, examining her hands. "I think the one you found was taken before the wedding. If you will notice her hands, she is not wearing the wedding ring and the engagement ring is still on the right hand."

Lauren leaned back, stunned by the discovery. Trying to process it all, she said, "The man with his arm around your great grandmother is my great great grandfather."

"Your great grandfather?"

"We think so, yes," she said.

They both sat back in their chairs, trying to figure out what this all meant when Dr. Higgins realized something, "You mentioned earlier that I have a copy of your great-great grandfather's book."

Lauren handed him the book she had not even realized she was still holding. "Yes, *Poor White Trash* was his most famous work. He wrote a few other books, but that was the big, famous one."

Looking at the dusty cover, Higgins said, "You know, I have never opened any of those older books over there. My grandfather gave them to me when I got my doctorate. He had said they were family heirlooms and had been in my great grandmother's book collection and had always been in her office. I keep them here as a remembrance of her. I got to know her growing up and she was the smartest person I ever met."

He closed his eyes for a moment, remembering his Great-Grand before looking at the book. Higgins opened the book to the title page when he saw the name of the author. Reading it out loud, he said, "Dr. James Pashen, Professor of Southern History, University of Virginia."

Dr. Higgins looked confused, "His name was James?"

"Yes," Lauren stated. "It's something of a family tradition to name the first boy James. In fact, my brother, my father, and my grandfather are all names James Williams, and if I ever decide to have kids, my first son will be James as well."

Higgins leaned forward and put his elbows on the desk. "Well, my grandfather was named James as well. He was my Great-Grand's first child."

He decided to look at the book, and began to look at the table of contents before deciding to flip through the book. As he was doing so, the book naturally fell open to page 316. Wedged between pages 316-317 was a worn out piece of paper folded and taped together. Dr. Higgins gingerly removed the paper, and opened it on the desk.

Lauren leaned over to get a good look at the paper, when her eyes widened with shock as she began to read...*My Dearest Julia.*

Printed in Great Britain
by Amazon